TOMORROW'S DREAMS

Nellie is a talented paintress in the pottery industry of the 1920s. Disaster strikes the family, and she becomes the main breadwinner for her parents and three siblings. But the fates conspire against her and she is forced to seek employment where she can find it. She loses her heart to the wrong man and he, recognising her special talents, offers her a future. But how could she ever move into his world?

CHRISSIE LOVEDAY

◆

TOMORROW'S DREAMS

Complete and Unabridged

LINFORD
Leicester

First published in Great Britain in 2011

First Linford Edition
published 2011

British Library CIP Data

Loveday, Chrissie.
    Tomorrow's dreams. - -
(Linford romance library)
1. China painters- -Fiction.
2. Great Britain- -Social conditions- -
20th century- -Fiction. 3. Love stories.
4. Large type books.
I. Title II. Series
823.9'2–dc22

ISBN 978–1–4448–0892–6

Published by
F. A. Thorpe (Publishing)
Anstey, Leicestershire

Set by Words & Graphics Ltd.
Anstey, Leicestershire
Printed and bound in Great Britain by
T. J. International Ltd., Padstow, Cornwall

This book is printed on acid-free paper

The Potteries, 1925

Nellie Vale sighed as she spread dripping on four thick slices of bread. Her two brothers and small sister were waiting anxiously for their share and snatched them as soon as she moved away.

'Leave that last one. It's mine, for my dinner. I'm just going up to see Mum, then I'll have to be off. Don't want to be in trouble for being late again.'

She ran up the steep stairs, already weary and the working day hadn't started yet. Her mother, Nan Vale, was still fast asleep, her breathing heavy and irregular. The rattle in her chest sounded worse than ever. Nellie wished there was something she could do to make her poor mum feel better, but the wretched bronchitis had hit her really hard this year. She heard the church clock chime seven and ran back down again.

'Now, our Lizzie,' she said to the four-year-old, 'I want you to see to Mum when she wakes up. There's some tea in the pot. Pour it carefully, half a cup, mind, and take it up to her.' The child nodded, her eyes enormous in the pinched little face. 'You two, get off to school. I don't want more trouble with them truancy people. Understand?'

'Yes, Nellie,' they chorused, looking as if butter wouldn't melt. They rarely went to school at all and Joe was just hanging on for the end of the year when he could get a job and earn some money of his own.

Nellie ran down the grimy street, avoiding the worst bumps in the cobbles. The air was thick with the fumes from the mines and the pot banks, the china factories that gave the entire area its characteristics. Fat bottle kilns belched out polluting smoke on the days they fired the china. The air had barely cleared before the next lot started all over again. If anyone asked the eighteen-year-old Nellie, she'd have said it was just the smell of the Potteries.

'Mornin',' she called to the lodge man, holding out her bag for his inspection.

'Morning, me duck,' he replied with a nod of approval. 'How's that mother of yours?'

'Bit poorly, but thanks for asking. Best get in or I'll be in trouble.'

'You're OK. Albert's gone up to the clay end to sort summat out.'

'Good job an' all. I'm out of breath after running all the way here. See you, George.'

He watched the skinny girl as she climbed the steps. 'She could do with a good feed herself,' he murmured.

She went into the decorating shop where a couple of the girls were sitting at their benches, mixing paints on the tiles they used. Nellie sniffed deeply. The smell of turps and paint were

3

familiar and comforting and she loved it.

'Come on, Dolly Daydream. Get the kettle on. I'm fair parched this morning. When you've done that, you can go next door and tell them we need another board of cups.'

'And no making eyes at that young Sidney. I've seen you looking at him.' The banter was good natured and the other workers smiled at the shy girl.

Nellie blushed and went down the icy steps to fill the kettle from the pump in the yard. She set it on the fire hob and picked up the mugs. Each member of the decorating shop brought their own enamel mugs into work, a privilege allowed solely to them, as they were among the elite of the factory.

She went into the workshop next door where the racks of glazed fine bone china waited for the paintresses to make them into the handpainted specialities of this world famous factory.

'Vera says to bring in another board of cups. And there's one finished in the paint shop ready to go down for firing.'

She rushed back to the kettle before it started boiling over and putting out the fire.

'Better make one for Albert. He'll be in soon,' Vera said. She was the senior paintress in the department and the only one who could really stand up to Albert and his roving hands.

The day went on. Nellie was sent on errands here and there and scarcely had time even to eat her slice of bread and dripping. But there was a lot of fun and laughter in the workshop as the group of women teased each other.

When the siren went at five o'clock everyone packed up for the day. It was Nellie's job to see that all the tiles the girls used to mix the paints were left clean. She made sure the tins of paint powder were properly sealed and stored back on the shelf. She swept the floor and sprinkled water down to lay the dust.

'Goodnight, Mr Albert,' she called through his office door.

''Night, Nellie. You're doing a good job, girl. When you're a bit older, you might get a chance to do a bit of painting yourself. Would you like that?'

'Oh, yes, sir. I'd love to have a go. Vera let me try on a broken cup with a bit of her spare paint one day. It's so exciting to see the lines looking like something special. Bet they look real pretty when they're finished.' In common with most of the workers, she had never actually seen the finished products.

'Aye, well, keep at it. 'Night Nellie.'

She ran off, happy enough to be a part of the factory and with the promise of a future. She almost forgot to show George her empty bag as she left. She couldn't imagine anyone actually stealing anything from the factory but it was an age-old custom that had to be followed. It was almost dark when she arrived home, exhausted. She wondered if anyone had brought in anything for tea.

Joe was sitting on the doorstep.

'What are you doing out here? You'll

catch your death.'

'We've got trouble. It's Dad. There's been an accident at the pit.'

'What sort of accident?'

'A bad sort,' Joe told her. Nellie's heart sank. As if there wasn't enough to cope with. Her mother couldn't manage the little ones and there was always too much work to do for one person. She pushed the door open and took in the scene with horror.

'Oh, our Dad, whatever have you done?'

'Bit of an accident. I came off lightly. Jake down the road, he's been hurt really bad. They say he's lost his leg and he's fighting for his very life now.' Enoch looked very pale and was in deep shock. He was feeling a mixture of relief that it wasn't him and guilt for thinking that way. 'Me, I've just hurt my hand. It'll be all right. Don't fret.'

'But how did you do it?'

'Got it trapped when I was trying to help get Jake out. There was a rock fall and we couldn't get out of the way fast enough.'

'But has anyone looked at it?'

'Oh yes. The medical officer came to the pit head right away. Trouble is, I'm laid off for a few weeks.'

'A few weeks?' Nellie almost yelled. 'It must be a bad injury. How on earth shall we manage for a few weeks?'

Enoch put his head in his hands.

'I don't know, ducks, and that's a fact. There's no welfare for the likes of us. We'll just have to manage on what you bring home. Maybe our Joe can get some work. He's near enough finished his schooling now.'

'Oh, Dad. Is Mum any better?'

'Not really. She tried to get up but then she got all dizzy and had to go back to lie down.'

'Is there anything in for tea?'

'I haven't looked. I was hoping you'd make something when you got home.'

Nellie sighed. It was the same every night. All she wanted to do was to sit down and put her feet up but it was rarely possible. She went round to the corner shop and collected a few things to feed the family. Luckily, they had a slate there, as did most of the customers. She would pay off the credit when she collected her wages on Friday evening and start a new slate at the beginning of the next week. They never caught up.

'I suppose you don't need a new errand boy, do you Mrs Parks?' she asked hopefully in the shop.

'What, you thinking of your Joe?' replied the shop owner with a sniff.

'Yes. Our dad's had a bad accident and been laid off for a few weeks. My mum's still poorly and there's only my wage coming in.'

'I'm really sorry, love, but your Joe's not the most reliable lad I know.' She paused and felt badly for the young girl in front of her. 'Oh, go on, then. I'll tell you what, I'll give him a go on Saturdays. Can't pay 'im much but it'll be a start. Tell 'im to call round on Friday evening.'

'Thanks ever so much, Mrs Parks. I really appreciate it.' She rushed home and told her brother the news. He looked a bit grumpy.

'It's me only day off,' he moaned.

'Lucky you. When do I get a day off? You just make sure you do a good job or there'll be even less food on the table.'

Over the next few days, there seemed no end to Nellie's problems. At least when her dad was home, he could look after Nan and little Lizzie and he did try his best to help round the house. She set off for work the next day with a heavy heart. She could see no end to their problems.

'Eh, Nellie. Glad you're early today,' Albert greeted her. 'Betty's gone off sick and we've got a big order to finish. Now's your chance to show me if you're any good with a paintbrush. Take a seat alongside Vera there. She'll show you what to do.'

'Thanks, Sir, thanks very much. It's just what I've always wanted. I won't let you down.'

'Right. Well, see as you don't.'

They shuffled round the work table so Nellie could have a seat. She took over Betty's tile and pot of brushes and watched carefully to make sure she was doing everything correctly. She took the little palette knife and carefully mixed paint powder with linseed oil.

'That's it, love,' Vera said approvingly. 'Get it really smooth. Mix the green paint on one side and the brown on the other. Keep the mix soft but not too runny. You can take a bit of each colour and blend it as you paint. I'll put one cup that I've done right next to you and I need to you copy the stems exactly the same on each cup. It's a very important job cos you're the first one to set the pattern right. Then Maggie does the leaves and finally, I do the roses themselves.'

'I see,' Nellie said, her hand shaking slightly. 'Like this?'

'Not quite. Wipe that off with a bit of rag. Don't let your hand shake or the stems will be all wobbly. Rest your hand on the bench as you work. That'll keep it steady.'

'I'm just a bit nervous. Hang on.' She wiped off the mess and carefully painted the line and filled in the stem with delicate strokes. Her tongue was sticking out and she was breathing heavily.

'I should use the brush, Nellie, not your tongue.' Nellie looked up and grinned back at Maggie's teasing.

'Give me a chance. This is the first time I've done this for real.'

'Well get a move on or we'll be waiting for you.'

'Now then, Maggie. You can always make the tea if you've got time on your hands,' Vera chided.

'All very well but we're on piece work. If we don't keep the numbers up, we'll all be light in our wage packets come the end of the week,' Florence moaned. She was not the most popular girl in the team and she sounded very grumpy.

By ten o'clock, Nellie was getting the

hang of her new role and was speeding up. She even asked if she might paint some of the leaves by the end of the day, but Vera was determined she needed to serve her unofficial apprenticeship.

'Don't try running when you're barely walking,' she was told. The others all accepted her as one of them and someone even offered her a humbug during the afternoon.

'We're the most important part of the line,' Vera had told her. 'The stuff that comes through here is all but finished and it's our work that determines if they're going to sell or not.'

However important she was feeling, Nellie still had to climb down the wooden stairs to the pump and get water to make the tea. She was the youngest there and besides, there was nobody else. But she did everything she was asked with good grace.

★   ★   ★

'So do you get more wages now, our Nellie?' asked Joe a few days later, after his sister had worked out the week.

'I think so. I can paint nearly a hundred stems in a day now.'

'Sounds really boring. Why can't you paint the whole thing?'

'Cos this is the way it's done. Once I've got better, I shall be able to do more of the processes. Now, go and get some more coal in, please. That fire won't cook anything and I need to do supper.' She tidied her fine blonde hair back into its usual bun at the nape of her neck and put on her apron. She looked and felt many years more than eighteen.

A Promotion For Nellie

It seemed a long winter and the family continued to suffer from extreme poverty. But despite it all, there was great love and support. The little ones adored their big sister and the stories she told them.

She remembered stories from her own school days and elaborated on them with great imagination. Enoch was still kept off work by a hand that never seemed to improve. He tried to use it when he could but it was stiff and painful and had little strength for anything much. He did try to help with keeping the home running but Nellie was still left to bear the brunt of everything. Though her mother was showing a little more life, she was unable to do very much before she began to cough again.

'Eh, I'm sorry you have to carry so much for this family,' Enoch said almost every day. 'You have little brothers and a sister to look after and a pair of useless parents.'

'Now Dad, don't talk like that. It's just a bad patch. We'll get through it.' She wished she believed her words. 'Good news is, I might be taken on as an official paintress. Means I shall get a better regular wage and if we work really fast, we get extra.'

'They've told me I might as well leave school right away,' Joe told them over supper.

'You must finish your schooling, lad. You're only just twelve.'

'There's nothing else they can teach me,' he said with a grin. 'Thought we could get me a job somewhere. Help out the family a bit. Now, how about another slice of bread for a working man?'

'We can see. Work's pretty scarce around here. You're a bit young for the mines just yet, but maybe there's something we can find.'

'You ain't workin' yet, our Joe. If you have another piece of bread, I want one as well,' piped seven-year-old Ben.

'Neither of you is having another slice. You won't get any breakfast if you do.'

'I'm sick of this,' Enoch said, thumping his good fist on the table. 'Never enough to eat and always fighting to pay the rent. We'll have to do something about it.' He strode out of the house, slamming the door behind him.

'Why's Dad shouting?' asked Lizzie timidly. She went and climbed on her big sister's knee. Nellie hugged her and tried to comfort the little girl. She was more of a mother to the child than their own sickly parent.

'He's worried about us all. Now, go and see if Mum's all right. She might like a drop more tea.'

At work, Nellie could forget about her dreary life at home and became enthralled by the designs that were being created by her fellow workers. Whole matching tea-sets were being made. The familiar rose pattern was covering plates, saucers, sugar and creams and her own skills were improving day by day.

When the rest of the girls took a lunch break one day, she moved round the bench to each place and completed the whole pattern on a saucer. Without time to dry between the different colours, it was slightly smudged, but Vera was very complimentary.

'You'll be putting us all out of work soon. You've got talent, lass. Takes some of us years to achieve what you've just done there. Go and show it to Albert. Reckon as he'll like what he sees.'

'Really? I thought you'd tell me off for using your places.'

Nellie grinned and her usual shyness was forgotten as she knocked on the manager's door.

'Excuse me, sir, but Vera says I should show you this. I did it all myself in the lunch break.'

'Very good. Not quite up to our standard but if you did the whole thing in one go, it suggests to me that you're ready to move on a bit. I know you were only filling in for Betty, but I've heard she isn't coming back. Expecting she is, and poorly with it. So you can have her place permanent, like. And we'll get someone else in to do the errands. You've got a sister, haven't you?'

'Well, yes, but she's only little. I've got a brother looking for a job. He's leaving school now.'

'Can't have a lad in the paint shop. The girls would make mincemeat out of him. Sorry, love.'

She went back into the work shop and told Vera the outcome.

'Thought he'd make it a proper appointment. Well done. Everyone, Nellie's one of us, permanent.'

'That's good,' Maggie said. 'You can celebrate by making a brew.'

'We're getting someone new to do

that,' Nellie told them. 'But I'll do it for now. Just to celebrate. Eh, does that mean I can paint the leaves now, Vera?' She laughed as she went down the steps to the water pump to fill the kettle. She'd have to get her own enamel mug now, instead of using the old chipped cup offered to the girl who made tea. She was now officially a paintress.

She was so happy with her new role that Nellie failed to notice the stirring of unrest at some of the other benches in the paint shop. Her own life had been confined to the bench with Vera and the others and she almost forgot there was a considerable number of other women in the department.

The most superior bench was the one used by the four gilders. It was their job to paint the gold rims on cups, saucers and plates, on the more expensive lines produced by the company. On some pieces, there were gold leaves and swirls to be added to the colours Vera and the others produced. Using the dark brown-looking paint that was magically changed to shining gold when it came out of the kiln, they considered themselves a cut above the rest.

'Nellie, go down to the stores and fetch us some more of the gold powder. You'll have to sign for it, of course, as it's so expensive. You can sign your name, can you?'

'Of course I can,' Nellie said angrily. 'But it isn't my job any more. I'm now a paintress and they're getting a new girl to do the running round.'

'Well, she isn't here yet, so get along with you,' Mathilda, the oldest of the group, snapped.

Nellie looked across at Vera, uncertain about what she was supposed to do. But her friend was concentrating on her work and hadn't noticed the slight problem that was building.

'Oh, all right. I'll get it this once but you shouldn't ask me again.' Matilda looked furious but smirked at her slight victory. There was a muttering around the bench but Nellie walked away, pretending not to notice. As she was coming back with the small tin of powder, Albert was coming out of the office.

'Where've you been?' he demanded.

'Fetching gold powder for Mathilda.'

'Not your job any more. You go back to your bench. I'll have a word.'

As she went, she heard the raised voices and glanced over to see a furious Mathilda arguing with the manager. The others looked over and then turned their gaze to Nellie.

'Everything all right, love?' Vera asked.

'Just running an errand for Mathilda and Mr Albert caught me. I wasn't sure what I should do. I'm so used to running after everyone, I just did it.'

'Well, now you're a lady of leisure you can start bossing someone around yourself,' Florence said with sneer that made Nellie wince slightly.

'No sign of much leisure in this place,' she said, trying to smile at the other woman.

'Depends who your friends are,

doesn't it? Once you're in with the boss, anything can happen.'

The chat went back and forth until Vera told them all to be quiet and get on with their work.

'Well, some of us have to work for years to get taken on permanent, like. Others can just waggle their hips and everything comes to them.' Florence was clearly very jealous of Nellie's apparent good fortune.

'She's not got much in the way of hips to waggle,' Maggie laughed. 'Proper skinny is our Nellie.' They all laughed and the tension was broken and work continued. All the same, Nellie was concerned that she might face a few problems in the future, but she was much too happy with her work to let it get her down.

One morning, Mr Albert came into the paint workshop and told them all to be quiet and listen.

'I want you all working extra hard today. None of your usual chatter and fooling around. We're getting the big bosses making a tour. Mr Henry Cobridge and his son, Mr James, are making an inspection right round the factory. Any nonsense from any of you and you're out on your ear. And no talking to them.'

'S'pose they ask us something,' Maggie said. 'Aren't we allowed to reply?'

'You answer with respect and don't forget to call them sir. Right. Get on with your work now.'

They all looked round whenever the door rattled. There was an air of nervous anticipation.

'I've heard Mr James is very good looking,' Maggie whispered.

'Now then,' Vera snapped. 'He's not going to be interested in the likes of any of us. Shush, now. They're coming.' Everyone's heads went down as they concentrated on working and scarcely dared to look up. Mr Albert came out of his office and stood smiling as if he owned the place. The girls couldn't hear what he was saying but whatever it was, the two men were showing great interest. They walked round, looking at each girl's work.

'You're new, aren't you?' Mr James asked Nellie.

'Quite new, sir,' she replied nervously.

'You're doing some good work. Well done.' He spoke for a few minutes to some of the others and smiled again at Nellie.

The two men left and a buzz of conversation rose after the doors were closed again.

'He's a bit of all right, that young one,' Maggie said. 'Reckon he liked you, Nellie.'

'Don't be daft. He just asked me stuff about my work.'

'Come on settle down again,' Mr Albert told them. 'You're not going to make the numbers this week at your present rate.

Her confidence increased both at work and at home. The extra wages helped and even Joe stuck at his job as errand boy for the corner shop.

Mrs Parks gave him some more deliveries to do and he handed over his pennies to Nellie with good grace when he came home from his work. The shopkeeper often gave him a few leftover vegetables on Saturday evenings to add to their weekend meals. Even their mother, Nan, seemed to be making some improvement and she was downstairs for the evening meal more often than not.

'We've got a plan,' announced Enoch one evening. 'Me and Joe, we're going to work together at the pit.'

'But how can you work with your damaged hand?' Nellie asked. 'I thought they wouldn't take you back unless you were fit again.'

'If we work side by side, the way many lads do with their fathers, Joe can cover for me when I need it. We've been to see Mr Osborne and he's willing to take us both on together. We start on Monday next week. I reckon we're climbing out of this black hole we've been living through. Our Nellie's well established at the pot bank and me and Joe will soon be working and earning a decent wage again.'

'And I'm feeling much better now,' Nan added. 'This is a new start for the Vale family.'

'Eh, I do hope so,' Nellie said joyfully. She even dared to hope she could take up an invitation from the other girls at work and go to one of the social club dances they all talked about. Mind you, that might be a while off, as she had nothing suitable to wear. Even her Sunday best had seen better days quite a few years back.

With more, better quality food on the table, the whole family began to look and feel better. Spring had arrived and Nan was managing to do more and more in the house. There was a meal ready most nights when they all came home from work and Nellie made them all laugh with her stories of the other girls at the factory.

'It's so good to hear you sounding

happy,' Nan told her daughter. 'You've had a hard time looking after us all and trying to make ends meet. And you might even be putting on a bit of weight at last.'

'That's cos I don't have to rush round all day. I sit at my bench all the time.'

'Well, it suits you to have bit of flesh on you. Always were a skinny little thing.'

'I might go for a bit of a walk,' Enoch announced, pushing his chair back after finishing his meal.'

'Can I come, Dad?' Ben asked hopefully.

'Sorry lad, not this time. Gotta bit of business to sort out.'

'You going to the club, Dad?' Joe suggested. 'Only I qualify to come with you now. I'm working down the pit, aren't I?'

'I don't want you getting into bad habits, Joe,' Nan said hastily. 'There's drink served down at that club and you know how I feel about drink.'

'We're not all in the Band of Hope, Mum. You might have signed the pledge but we haven't. Besides, I want to get to know some of my mates. I never see them outside work.'

'What's the Band of Hope?' Ben asked. 'Do they play music and stuff?'

'No, love. It's through the chapel I joined. They ask us all to sign the pledge. To promise you'll never touch drink. There's too many families destroyed by drink. Not just the men. Some of the women, too, drink strong liquor and then use all their money so they get into debt and worse.'

'Come on, Nan. Just a jar or two with the lads doesn't hurt. Man deserves it after a day down in that hell hole. You don't know what it's like.'

'Oh, please yourself. But don't let our Joe drink anything he shouldn't. He's only twelve, don't forget.'

'Mum,' the lad protested. 'I work hard enough, don't I?'

'How's it going, you and Dad working side by side?' Nellie wanted to know.

'S'all right. Dad still can't lift much so I have to do quite a lot on my own. We've worked out a way of hiding it so the foreman doesn't catch on.'

The young man and his father left the house and the youngest children went to bed. Nellie and her mum sat by the fire, chatting comfortably.

'Shall we have another brew? I reckon the leaves in the pot'll stand another drop of water.' Nellie swung the blackened kettle over the fire on its little stand and watched as it started to boil. The brown teapot had more water added to the sludge of tea leaves and it was left to brew.

'There's not much milk left so be sparing with it.'

They sat hugging the mugs of almost orange tea, coloured by the sterilised milk favoured by the family. It tasted bitter but it was hot and refreshing.

'There's one girl who doesn't like me much,' Nellie continued her tale. 'She's called Florence and she's jealous that I got made up to full paintress so soon.

She took months before they let her have her own tile and brushes. I don't trust her, but the others are all good so I'm happy enough.'

'I never realised there was so much standing put on it. I s'pose it's all to do with earnings, when it comes down to it.'

'But we're working together. It's piece work so we all have to pull our weight. If we don't get the targets, all our pay packets are bit light. Strikes me the best girls are the ones who make everyone's pay turn out right.'

'And you're one of the best ones, I take it?'

'Course I am.' She laughed.

'Well, just watch out. I know how nasty some of these girls can be. Now, I'm going to wash the pots and take myself off to bed. I just hope our Joe doesn't come home too late to work properly tomorrow. Last thing we can do with is him getting the sack. I can't face going back to the way things were.'

For the next few weeks, all seemed to

be going well for Nellie and the rest of the family.

'You're coming on a treat,' Vera told her. 'You want to have a go at doing something else? We've got a load of new patterns to learn so if you like, you can make a start.' She showed her some sketches which had been shaped to fit round the edges of plates. 'We have to do three of these on each plate. These are for side plates, you know, bread and butter plates, so they're quite small. Fit them round the edge, spaced equally. Like with the roses, start by doing the stems to get the patterns set.'

Nellie began the new work with great enjoyment. This was a pattern using primroses and violets, linked together with trails of stems and leaves. She worked meticulously to begin with, scared of making a mistake and getting put back on her old work. After the first few, she tried putting in the flowers and leaves and gradually, built up the whole pattern.

'Is that right, Vera?' she asked anxiously.

'Great job. Well done.'

Everything was going very well and Nellie was getting better and better and speeding up, too. The other girls at her bench were pleased to see the girl progressing so well. It also helped them with their numbers by the end of the week, so pay packets were looking good.

'Why can't I have a go at something different?' moaned Florence one day. 'It isn't fair that she should get to work on all the new patterns. I've been here much longer than that Nellie Vale.'

'She can do it and you can't,' snapped Maggie.

'Who do you think you are, bossing me around?'

'All right, all right,' Vera interrupted. 'Finish that batch, Flo, and you can have a change as well. But watch we don't fall back on numbers. I've got bills to pay at the end of the week.'

There were still a few moans from

Florence, but she speeded up her work and finished her allotted tasks. Over the next few days, some of Nellie's things seemed to get into the wrong places. Her own brushes went missing and one of the other girls lost her favourite brush, only to find it in Nellie's pot.

Several times, the powdered colours had lids removed and left on the shelf, always the colours Nellie had been using. She knew she would never have left them uncovered as the paints deteriorated. After all her years of being the errand runner, she knew it was more than her life was worth to leave the lids off. Lots of other little problems occurred and Nellie was usually the victim. She tried to ignore it and continued working as well as she could.

Florence was spending time in Mr Albert's office, usually making an excuse to take in his tea or to fetch something. She even sat on his desk, laughing and joking. Maggie was annoyed and in turn, complained to Vera.

'There's nowt I can do about it. If Mr Albert wants her in there, I'm not going to be the one to complain. You know what he's like. Maybe I can have a word. If he's making advances, maybe she does need a bit of my advice.'

But far from needing advice, Florence was actively encouraging the boss to take an interest and began to take advantage of it. She got herself a small promotion and took over as unofficial foreman of one of the other benches. None of the girls at Vera's bench were unhappy at the change and a new girl joined them, happy to be working at all.

Florence stayed late several times a week and Mr Albert took to walking her home, often via the local pub. Nobody dared complain about anything or it got back to the boss and everyone knew who was responsible for that. If anyone said anything out of turn, they were called into Mr Albert's office and often came out crying. Nellie had always worked hard tried her best to keep out of trouble. She had never complained when the problems had occurred and the others had accepted her apologies, even when she didn't feel it was her fault. She was upset when she was called into the office before the end of work one Friday.

'I'm very disappointed in you, Nellie. I thought you were going to be one of my best workers but you've let me down. After I promoted you so soon, as well. Not good enough, you know.'

'I'm sorry but what have I done?'

'All these stupid tricks you've been playing. Messing with the other girls' things. Being careless. Putting cracked china with the good stuff to be fired.'

'But I never. I haven't broken a single thing since I've worked here.'

'Don't make it worse by lying. You're the only one working on the primrose and violet line. There were three chipped plates in the last lot you sent down.'

'But there couldn't have been. I'd never try to hide it if I'd seen a crack or anything. There are standards here, sir.

I always try to keep them high.'

Mr Albert frowned. How could he believe her? He'd seen the evidence with his own eyes. Three chipped plates. Admittedly, he been surprised when they were pointed out to him but the faults were there and as Nellie had been the only paintress to be doing that size and pattern, it had to be her fault.

'I don't know what to say to you. You're a good worker. A talented girl. But the plates were chipped and put out after you'd finished them. We always take out anything cracked before you get your hands on them. One more cracked painted item and you can collect your cards.'

'Thank you, sir, for the chance. It won't happen again.' She held her head high. Nobody was going to see how near to tears she was. Vera and Maggie went over to her and asked what was the problem. When she told them, they were so kind that Nellie couldn't hold back her tears this time.

'I wouldn't put cracked or chipped ware in the firing basket. Honest I wouldn't. I'm always so very careful.'

'I know you are, love,' Vera told her. 'Come on now, dry your eyes. It's all but time. Clean off your tile and brushes and we'll start to pack up.' The older woman knew that it wouldn't have been Nellie's fault, but she said nothing.

Nellie spent a miserable weekend worrying about Mr Albert's threat. She knew she was innocent and suspected that it must all be Florence's doing. She was the boss's pet and was always telling tales. Besides, she had never liked Nellie and so it seemed her jealousy had now got the better of her. Nan was worried about her daughter's mood and disappointed that she would say nothing about what was troubling her. When Monday came, Nellie set off to work with a heavy heart.

'Morning, George,' she said as cheerfully as she could to the lodge man. No use inflicting her troubles on to anyone else.

'"Allo love. You getting on all right?'

'Not bad, thanks.'

'I hear your brother's working now. Saw 'im down the club with your dad. Must make things a bit easier at home.'

'Yes, thanks. We're doing fine now. Cheerio then, George.'

'Bye, love.' He had a soft spot for the skinny girl.

'Morning, love,' Vera greeted cheerily. 'Had a good weekend?'

'Not bad. Went to the chapel with me mum, but didn't do much else. Now, what am I on today?'

'You're back on stems. Mr Albert wants you on something safe.'

'Oh, but what about the primroses and that?'

'They've gone to Flo's bench. No, don't say owt. I know it's unfair, lass, but we has to take it. She's got herself cosied up with him and that's that.' Vera was clearly unhappy but she could do nothing. They settled down to work.

39

Halfway through the week, everyone was bored and they had done fewer pieces that usual. Once more, Nellie was chosen for an interview with Mr Albert.

'Right, now, Nellie Vale. What have you got to say for yourself? I gave you a chance last week but you've let me down again.'

'I'm sorry but what have I done this time?'

'Your attitude has put everyone off. We're way down on output. I can only think it's you grumbling that's turned everyone off their work so I have no alternative but to give you your cards. You'll get your pay to the end of this week and then you can go.'

'But I haven't done anything wrong. I haven't said anything. I've been working like I always do.'

'It's your bench that's down. And I've heard about your attitude. A little bird keeps me informed of all the goings on. Now, get out. I don't want to hear another word or you can go right away without any more pay.'

White-faced and trembling, Nellie tottered out of the office. Florence was smirking and laughing with her little group across the room but looked away when Nellie stared. Vera immediately took hold of Nellie's hand and asked what had happened.

'He's only gone and given me me cards. Says I've put everyone off working with my grumbling. But I haven't said anything, have I? Says the production's way down on normal.'

'We're up to the usual numbers, aren't we?' asked Maggie.

'Course we are,' Vera reassured her girls. 'It's one of the other benches letting the side down. I reckon they've bitten off more than they can chew. Can't manage the difficult pieces and so they've slacked off.'

'And we can all guess who that is, can't we?' Maggie was almost shouting in her anger. 'We won't put up with it, will we, girls?'

'Shut up, Maggie,' Vera cautioned. 'I

don't know how our numbers have been fiddled, but that's what's happened. We'll meet after work and talk about it. Pass the word round to the other benches. Not to you-know-who, though.'

'Where shall we meet?'

'Better not be too close to the gates. Down Beswick Street. There's a patch of rough ground. We can meet there right after work. We can't have someone sacked because of tale tattling.'

'But, Vera,' Nellie began, 'I don't want any of you to . . . '

'Be quiet. We're not going to stand for bullying of any kind. Just be in Beswick Street after work.'

The group of women, all wearing headscarves and winter coats assembled on the patch of ground. There were all slightly nervous, wondering what was happening. Vera stood at the front and raised her arm to get silence.

'Thanks for coming, girls. As several of you know, our Nellie here has been given the sack this afternoon. It's all most unfair and nothing to do with the quality of her work. I'd go as far as to say that next to me, she's possibly the best new girl we've ever taken on. Why has she been given the sack, you'll be wondering? It's because someone has taken against her. Jealous of her talent and her promotion, she's spread lies and rumours.'

Vera paused as there was a rumbling of anger among the assembled group. 'Well, we don't feel it's right and I'm going to ask you all to down tools for a an hour tomorrow. I'll tell Mr Albert the reason for the stoppage and demand he reinstates Nellie. Now, are you with me?'

There was a unanimous shout of, 'Yes.'

'Right. That's settled then. We'll work till nine o'clock and then down tools. I'll go in to see him and explain our terms. See what he says. If he says no, we'll start work again exactly one hour later and have another down tools at eleven.'

'How will you know the time? We usually have to go by the siren.' This was the sound that signalled start times, lunch and finishing time siren fixed to the top of one of the bottle kilns in the yard.

'I'll bring in our clock from the mantelpiece at home. Right then, see you all at work tomorrow.'

'Oh Vera, I don't know what to say. I hope there's no more trouble after tomorrow. It's very good of you to care so much but I don't want to cause trouble for everyone else.'

The older woman put a hand on Nellie's arm and used a wonderful Potteries phrase. 'Dunner fash the' sen, lass,' meaning don't worry yourself.

A Joyous Christmas

The atmosphere was tense in the decorating shop. Everyone was looking at each other, waiting for a signal. Florence was sitting in what had become her usual place on Mr Albert's desk, drinking tea with him. She had her back to the rest of the girls and was laughing and evidently joking. Promptly at nine o'clock, at a signal from Vera, the girls all put down their brushes and folded their arms.

'What?' Mr Albert squawked, shoving Florence aside. 'What's going on? Do you know owt about this?' Florence looked round in alarm. She had no idea what was happening. 'What the heck's going on?'

Vera stood up. 'We're striking until you take Nellie back on. She's one of the best workers you've got and she's been treated badly. She isn't guilty of any of the stuff you said. It's someone else making mischief.' The girls applauded as Vera sat down.

'Oh, yes, and who do you say that might be?'

'Not mentioning any names. But it isn't Nellie.'

'You daft lot. You don't know what you're talking about. Now get back to work.'

They sat in a silent, sullen row at their benches and not a single one picked up their brushes. Even the girls at Florence's bench were sitting staring. They hadn't quite downed tools but nor were they working. Florence sidled past the boss, touching his arm gently as she went. He pushed her away.

'Come on, girls, be reasonable. I know you're upset about Nellie's failure, but it's her own fault. She broke the china and tried to get away with it.' There was stunned silence. The girls looked at Nellie, who shook her head.

'I never broke anything. Someone was just trying to make me look careless. I don't know why it is that they took against me and I appreciate you all trying to help me but I'm not guilty of any of it.'

Mr Albert went back into his office and then came back to the door.

'You've got five minutes to get back to work.'

'You've got fifty minutes to take Nellie back,' Vera shouted and the girls all cheered. The boss went back into his office and slammed the door. Florence went to open his door but he waved her away.

'Stop crawling to the boss, Florrie. We all know who's responsible for this.'

'You don't know what you're talking about. You're all jealous just because I'm more popular.'

'Yes, we all know why. We don't know why you're so jealous of Nellie unless it's just that she's better at the job.'

The arguments went on until Mr

Albert came out of his office with a face like thunder.

'Right, you lot. Get back to work right now or you'll all have your cards by the end of the day. Nellie, come in here, right now.' They watched through the window in the office door as Nellie stood tall, her head held high. She said something they couldn't hear and then she turned and came out. She untied her pinny and collected several things from her bench. She walked to the main door of the paint shop and turned to address the whole group.

'Thank you all for your support and being such good friends but I'm going now. You might as well get back to work. If you don't, he's going to fire the lot of you. I'm off before he does.'

'Eh, Nellie love, I'm so sorry. But think about it. He wouldn't get any work done if he sacks us all. He'd never find enough talented paintresses in time, so he can't really threaten us like that. He's the one who'll look daft.'

'It's not worth it. If he doesn't find a

reason to sack me this time, he'll soon find another. You can't afford the bother of keeping me here. I'll find something else. And thanks again to all of you. Nearly all of you,' she added, glaring at Florence. 'And Vera, you've been a good friend. Take care. Bye, everyone.'

She stood outside the gates of the factory where she had worked for the last four years. The bottle kilns were smoking from the top as the new batch of china was being fired.

It surely wouldn't be long before she found another position. They'd all said she had talent. She went across to the canal on the other side of the road and sat to eat her sandwich. She had to think what to say to her mum and the rest of them.

Wanting to put it off as long as she could, she walked into Burslem and looked into the shop windows. There was a big china shop and she thrilled to see some of her own china in there. The rose pattern she knew so well in its unfinished state, looked beautiful, the full tea set, complete with the gilded rims, all set out on a lace table cloth. What must it be like to be rich enough to own something so beautiful?

She walked the three miles back to her home and went into the backdoor.

'Hello, love. You're back early.' Nan was in the kitchen, washing potatoes for supper. 'Everything all right?'

'No, Mum. I've been given me cards.'

'Oh no, our Nellie. Why?' She wiped her hands on her apron and sat down heavily.

Nellie explained what had been happening, and still protested her innocence.

'The other girls were wonderful, but I couldn't risk them losing their jobs, could I? So I walked out. Don't worry, I'll soon get another job. I'll start looking tomorrow. They all say how I'm a really good worker and talented at the job. All, that is, except Mr Albert and his little pet, Florence.'

'She sounds a right nasty piece of

work. Sit down now and we'll have a cuppa. I'll just put the spuds into the oven. We've got a nice stew for dinner tonight.'

'Sounds good. Better make the most of it while we've still got some decent money coming in.'

Enoch was less understanding when he arrived home. He shouted at her for being so stupid as to lose her job. She gritted her teeth and held her head up, refusing to let anyone see how upset she was.

'The girl causing all the mischief was the boss's little pet. I'm sure you know what I mean. I shall start looking for another job tomorrow. Don't fret.'

'You bet you will. And don't bother to come home till you've found something.'

Nellie set out early the next day. She walked round to several of the big pottery factories nearby, asking if they had any vacancies.

As soon as she mentioned her previous place of work, doors were shut in her face. She asked why and soon learned that Mr Albert and his friend, Florence, had spread the word that she was a trouble-maker.

Angrily, she walked to the next company but met the same result. Her name had been blacklisted. However unfair it all was, she was never given the opportunity to defend herself. She spent a couple of coppers on catching a bus into Stoke, hoping she might have luck a bit further afield. It would mean longer working hours if she did get a job there and extra expense in getting to work, but she couldn't do much about it.

The problem was always the same. Without references, nobody would look at her. She was always honest about the reasons she had left her previous place and quickly learned that honesty was not the best policy.

'I could work for a few days for nothing to prove myself,' she offered to one manager.

'Sorry, love, but from what I hear,

you're a bit of a risk.'

'Can I ask why you think so? Has someone been talking about me?'

'Happened to have a drink with a friend. Albert. He was your manager, wasn't he? He told me as you'd organised a strike. Now, I have to get on. Sorry.'

'Thanks, sir. I'm sorry, too.' She walked out, her head held high. She refused to be broken and kept her pride intact. She went back to her own area near Fenton and looked in the shop windows for postcards left there by people offering work. There were several asking for cleaners or girls to do washing in larger houses. Once more, references were a problem and she realised that somehow, she had to get someone to write a note for her. Mrs Parks from the corner shop looked a possibility.

'Do you think you could write me a reference?' she asked the kindly woman before she gave up her search for the day.

'I suppose I could, but you realise you haven't done any work for me. It might not count for much.'

'The thing is, I was unfairly dismissed from the potbank. It's the only job I've ever had apart from looking after the family. If you could just write that I'm a hard worker and that I'm honest, I'm sure that would help.'

'You're certainly a hard worker and I think that you're honest enough. I've known you since you were a little 'un so I dare say I can truthfully say I think you're as honest as can be. All right, love. I'll write you a reference. Seems a shame you have to look for a cleaning job when you've got talent as a paintress.'

'Thank you, Mrs Parks. I'm glad you understand. I hope I'll get back to painting one day.'

★ ★ ★

After a long trudge around, she finally secured a job as a cleaner in a local bakery. It was poorly paid and meant working in the evening, but at least it was something. It was soul-destroying work but she managed to survive it for a few weeks.

All the time, she was looking for other work but without luck. She was offered more work in the bakery, washing and ironing overalls. The pay was still pitiful but she took it on, knowing that every penny helped the family. Her hands became roughened and were often red and sore. She would be in no state for the delicate work of painting china if this continued for much longer.

'I don't like to see you working so hard for so little money,' Nan said one evening. Her daughter looked thinner than ever, despite eating a bit better. She sometimes brought a bun or two home, given to her by the baker for her lunch.

She always saved it for her brothers and sister and rarely ate any of it herself. Much of Joe's earnings went into the family pot, but they had debts to pay off so the family were little better off than before. As Christmas got closer, Nan knew it was going to be a poor affair this year.

'I was thinking about Christmas,' Nellie said.

'That's funny. I was thinking the very same thing myself today.'

'You can hardly miss it. Even Mrs Parks has got trimmings hanging up in the shop. And the butcher has all sorts of birds and things hanging outside. Be nice if we could have something special. What do you think?'

'I've been paying a few coppers into the club each week. But I reckon it won't buy much more than a piece of pork or maybe we might manage a chicken.'

'The baker's got some wonderful Christmas cakes. And he's making mince pies. I smell them cooking when I'm doing the ironing. Makes your mouth water, it does. I might see if we can have something special nearer the time. He might let me have something instead of some of my wages, if that's all right with you, Mum?'

'That sounds lovely, dear. Don't worry, I'm sure we'll manage something a bit special.'

Two days before Christmas, the baker came up trumps and handed Nellie a box as she was leaving for the day.

'Open it when you get home, love. I've packed it safe for you to carry. Our little thank you for your hard work.'

Excitedly, Nellie put the box on the kitchen table and she and her mum lifted the greaseproof paper covering the contents. There were six mince pies, some gingerbread biscuits and at the bottom a beautiful fruit cake, covered in glacé cherries and almonds.

'Oh, my goodness. I've never seen a cake like that in our house. What a kind man your boss is.'

'Makes all the hard work worth it, doesn't it? Better hide it away for the next two days. You know what our lot are like. Don't tell them about it, Mum, or it won't be special for Christmas Day.'

'It's going to be a good one, isn't it?' Nan said. 'I've managed to order a chicken for us. And I've made a plum pudding. Mrs Parks let me have some dried fruit a bit cheaper. I'm really looking forward to it. After last year, it seems like a miracle. Even your dad says he'll come to the chapel Christmas morning.'

One more day for them all to work and it was Christmas. There were small presents for each of the children, including Nellie. Lizzie had drawn a picture for her beloved sister and Nan had bought her a new bag.

'Oh, Mum, it's lovely. But you shouldn't have spent your money like that.'

'I got it on the club. You know, the one Mrs Parks helps run. You deserve it, love. You've helped hold this family together all these months. It's thanks to you that I got back on my feet again.'

Lizzie had a new rag doll and Ben had a football. Joe, now the working man himself, had a new warm scarf. Nan had knitted this herself with wool from an old sweater that had seen better days.

The sermon at the chapel had Lizzie wriggling on the uncomfortable seats after just a few minutes. They had enjoyed the singing of carols, but too much talking was more than the little girl could manage. Nellie played finger games with her, only half listening to the minister.

'And so, at this joyous time of giving,' he droned, 'I want you to think of those less fortunate. The Band of Hope and the chapel are planning an outing this year. The first Saturday in June, we are taking all the youngsters from the poor families of the parish to Rhyl for the day. Yes, a whole day at the seaside. There will be a picnic and we shall travel by train. Now, isn't that something to look forward to? I mention it today because we shall all have to work very hard to raise enough money for the venture.'

'Am I going to the seaside?' asked Lizzie in too loud a voice.

'You'll have to wait and see,' Nellie whispered back. 'We might not be one of the families.'

At last the service drew to a close and everyone shook hands with the Minister as they left the somewhat gloomy building.

'I shall be relying on you, Mrs Vale, to help with fund-raising for this outing. I expect your family will want to join in as well.'

'Oh dear, I'm not sure I can do much fund-raising,' Nan said. 'We hardly ever have even a copper or two left over each week.'

'I'm sure something will come of it. Happy Christmas to you all. Nice to see you with the family, Mr Vale.'

'Yes. Er, yes sir. Thank you.' Enoch was most ill at ease and could hardly wait to get away from the whole business.

The smell of roasting chicken filled the house when they all got back.

'Now then, there's just the veg to be done and we'll be ready to eat in about an hour. You all get out of my way, except you, Nellie. I shall need you to help. I've got the pudding steaming, but you can make the gravy.' She bustled about, giving Nellie a string of instructions.

'I might just go down to the Miners' Club for a quick drink while you're all busy with women's stuff.'

'Now, our Enoch, don't you go drinking strong liquor. This is still the Lord's day and you should respect it.'

'I'll go and keep me dad company,' Joe announced. 'I'll make sure he's back in time.'

'Mind you're not late, then.' They escaped quickly and Nan shook her head. 'I don't know what's worse. Having them under my feet all the time or worrying about them boozing. Now, there's carrots need peeling, love.'

For once, the family were able to eat

as much as they wanted and when the cake came out at tea-time, there were gasps all round.

'Eh, our Nellie, if I'd known you could cook something like that I'd have sent you to work in the baker's months ago.' They all laughed as the girl protested she'd had nothing to do with it.

'Mind you, he did have a beautifully ironed overall to work in. That must have made all the difference.'

Enoch's Selfish Behaviour

In the middle of March, Nellie had another blow. The kindly baker was forced to give her notice.

'I'm sorry, love, you've been a great worker, but I can't afford to keep you on. My missus is going to have to do the cleaning and washing. It's just the way things are. Money's tight all round. I'll keep you to the end of the week and you can count on a good reference. Hard worker like you'll soon find something else.'

'But I thought you were pleased with me. I've been working hard enough, haven't I?'

'Course you have, love. I'd like to keep you on, but things are bad. Takings are right down. Well, you must know the situation down the pits.

Miners are all on lower wages. Upshot is, it means we lose customers and takings go down. Just selling bread loaves doesn't make enough in a week. It's the cakes and fancies that bring in better profits.'

'I hadn't realised.' It was always a sign of higher status if you could afford shop-bought cakes, unless of course, there was a proper cook like there was in some of the posher establishments.

Regretfully, at the end of the week, she collected her final wages and a slip of paper with a reference written out in the baker's untidy scrawl. Nellie wondered of it might do more harm than good when she was looking for another job.

Inevitably, Enoch had a lot to say when he heard the news.

'What is it with you, girl? You get a good job and just when it's beginning to pay off, you get the sack.'

'It wasn't my fault.'

'It never is. What was it this time? Someone telling tales again?'

'No, Dad. The baker isn't selling as much as he was. You know yourself the miners are on lower wages.'

'Well, you'll have to find something. And be quick about it.'

Nellie sighed. It was always the same. According to her father, it was her fault whenever the family found itself in difficulties. She saw her father grimace when he moved his arm.

'What's up, Dad? Is your arm still paining you?'

'Course it is. Don't know where I'd be without our Joe. He's working much harder than he should be for a lad of his age.'

Lying on her bed that night, Lizzie cuddled up to her as always, Nellie tried to think of something she could do. Work was scarce all round. It was a bad prospect and she had to face an angry Enoch across the table every meal time. It was not good.

She asked everyone she knew if they needed any help in the house. When that failed, she began knocking on doors of the larger houses nearby.

She often thought of her days as a paintress and longed for the smell of turps and linseed oil again. She even wondered if she might call on Vera one day and see how things were going at the factory but her courage failed her.

Though Nan's health was much better on the whole, she had been wearing a frown most days lately, Nellie had noticed.

'What's up, Mum?' she asked. 'You've always got a frown on your face these days.'

'I'm worried about this Band of Hope trip to the seaside. We've hardly raised any money yet and there's only a couple of months to go.' It seemed like a century ago that the minister had made the announcement on Christmas Day.

'We didn't think things would go downhill like they have. It was a lovely Christmas, wasn't it?' The memory of the magnificent cake still lingered in her mind. 'So what are the plans for the outing?'

'We're trying to get up a fete and gala the Saturday after Easter. We can have a little parade of fancy dress for the kiddies and some stalls selling things people can make. Bring and buy stall. Hoopla. You know the sort of thing.'

'Sounds like a lot of work. Good job I've got time on my hands, isn't it? I could do some pictures for sale. Everyone says I'm good at drawing and painting. If I had some paints, that is.'

'That's an idea. You know, I think there may be an old paint box somewhere. Your grandad used to do a bit of painting many years ago. I'll see if I can lay my hands on them.'

For the next few days, Nellie was almost happy again. She loved doing her paintings and hoped they would be able to sell some of them at the fete. She was going out to do some errands for a local lady, Mrs Machin, and she told her about the fete. She had a small box of things ready for her when she came back from the shops one afternoon.

'Here you are, dear. A few things I don't need. There are some tablecloths and napkins and one or two ornaments. I don't know if you're having one of the jumble sale things, but I may be able to look out a few items of clothing. Do you think they might be of use?'

'I'm not sure what's being planned. But it's very kind of you. Can I ask my mother and let you know?'

'Of course. Though I don't go to chapel myself, I know they are trying hard to get rid of the drinking habits of the working classes. Many families are being destroyed by the menfolk wasting money that way.'

Nellie smiled. 'Yes, we're all doing our best. I've been busy painting some pictures to sell.'

'Really? I didn't know you had talent that way.'

'I was a paintress at the Cobridge factory before I . . . well, at one time.' Before she could stop herself, she found

68

herself telling the kindly lady about her unfair dismissal and the family's difficulties.

'How every distressing for you. I'm so sorry, dear. I'll tell you what, why don't you bring some of your pictures for me to look at? I may see one I'd like and that would be a start for your fund-raising. My friend, Mrs Cope, will be here, too.'

'Oh, thank you so much. I can bring some round later today if you like.'

'Very well. Now, how about making us a cup of tea? You can tell me some more about your family. You sound an interesting group.'

Excitedly, Nellie told her mother the news and showed her the box of things she had been given.

'And she says she's got some clothes if we want them. Do you think my paintings are good enough to show her?'

'Give it a go, love. You never know. Maybe it's the start of something for you. You might become an artist.'

'Come on, our Mum, who ever heard of a girl like me being an artist? I've seen proper pictures hanging up in some of the houses I've worked in but never anything like I can do. They're huge and usually painted in oil paints, not watercolours.'

'Well, I think they're lovely. That little picture you did of our Lizzie is as good as one of them photographs you see in the papers.' It was a little pencil sketch she had done one night when Lizzie had fallen asleep resting on a cushion on the floor.

'I like it too, but nobody else would want anything like that.' All the same, Nellie remained in a state of excitement until the meal was over and once more, she walked the mile or so to her potential customer's home.

'They are charming, dear,' Mrs Cope told her, as she looked through the heap of watercolours. 'You really do have some talent. Have you thought of going to an art school to learn a little more about technique?'

'I couldn't do anything like that. Besides, I'm not sure what this techni . . . thing is? I can't afford to buy anything to do with art. I only use my grandad's old paint set.'

'Technique is nothing you can buy, my dear. Now, I quite like this one. How much do you want for it?'

'I don't know. What do you think it's worth?'

'I'll pay you ten shillings for it. That should help you make a lot of money for the children's outing.'

'Ten shillings?' squeaked the girl. 'I'm not worth that much. That's as much as I earned in a whole week.'

'I'm not saying it's worth ten shillings. I'm saying it's what I will give you. There's a difference.'

'Thank you, Mrs Cope. Thank you ever so much.'

She practically skipped all the way home and burst into the kitchen.

'Mum, Dad, you'll never guess what? Mrs Cope has given me ten whole shillings for that painting. You know, the one with roses like the china cups I used to paint.'

'That's wonderful, our Nellie. What a start for the fund-raising.'

'You're never giving away all that money. Two shillings to the fund maybe. You can hand over the rest to me. It can go to the family pot.'

'You can't do that, Dad. Mrs Cope gave it to the fund-raising because she wants to help fight the demon drink.'

Enoch looked furious. He held his hand out for the precious note and Nellie looked at her mother for support, but Nan's eyes were firmly fixed on the fire. She was staring at it as if it was about to explode.

'Hand it over. I'll go and get some change at the club and you can have it for your blinkin' outin'. Waste of time if you ask me.'

'Dad,' Nellie was pleading. 'Please. You can't spend someone's charity money down at the Miners' Club.'

'Who says? Anyway, I'll have to have a pint if I'm to get them to give me

72

change. You coming down, our Joe? Drinks are on Nellie.' Gleefully, he grabbed his cap from the peg on the door and left the family staring at him. Joe looked uncomfortable.

'It's all right. I'm not going, so stop looking at me like that, our Nellie. If you must know, I think you're right, but there's no telling our Dad that. Besides, I'm fair worn out. I'm doing the work of two men. Dad can't hardly use one arm at all but he won't admit it. I have to cover for him as well as doing my own stint. The pit owners are making us work harder than ever and even though there's increased productivity, as they call it, we're not getting as much money as we did. I think he's upset by that and that's why he's going down to the club more and more.'

Nellie was lying in her bed fretting over the whole business. There was never any arguing with her father. He was always right, even when he was wrong.

She heard the church clock strike two

before he came back home. There were several crashes as he stumbled up the stairs and she heard him swearing a couple of times. Lizzie stirred but didn't wake.

She wondered if there was any of her precious money left for the outing. She had little idea of what went on at the Miners' Club, but from the little Joe had told her, she could imagine her father treating everyone who came in. Mrs Cope was right. Drink was a demon, right enough.

'Did Dad bring back any of my money?' she asked her mother next morning after the men had gone to work. Nan had dark rings under her eyes from lack of sleep.

'Course he did, love.'

'How much?'

'Well, enough to rattle in the tin when we start out on the stall.'

'How much?'

'One shilling and sixpence.'

'So where's the rest?'

'He's given me an extra shilling for

the house keeping.'

'And he's drunk the rest. Treated all his mates, I suppose. Sometimes I hate him. He never used to be like this. I daren't think what Mrs Cope would say, after her being so generous for the children.'

'He's a good man really, Nellie. He's had a hard time of it since the accident. He's never hit any of us. More than you can say for plenty of the men around here.'

'Hit us?' Nellie was aghast at the thought. But when she thought about it, many of the wives and families were mistreated by their menfolk. 'Well, I'm not letting him get his hands on my pictures nor any of the money they raise either here or at the fete and gala.'

It was raining the morning of the fete. Disappointed ladies collected at the gates of the big house that had offered the garden for the event. Boxes and bags containing items to be sold were soaking up water and the contents likely to be strewn over the path. The

Mine Captain's wife came out, an umbrella over her neatly coiffured hair.

'I'm so sorry. It's very disappointing for you. I've been in touch with the minister and he suggests the chapel hall should be used. I'll put up a sign on the gate and make sure everyone knows where it's being held.'

'Thank you, ma'am,' Nan said. 'It's such a shame though. There won't be much room for anything and the children's fancy dress parade will have to be cancelled. Our Lizzie and Ben will be that disappointed. They've been working on making themselves look like a couple of ghosts with some sheets for the last two days.'

'Perhaps it will dry up later and you can use the grass outside the chapel hall.'

'Right. Well, thanks anyway, ma'am, We'd best get down there and see about getting set up.'

At two o'clock sharp, the doors of the chapel hall were opened and a crowd flocked in looking for bargains. At two-thirty, the sun came out and people went outside to set up some of the games they had planned.

All in all, it had been a successful and enjoyable day.

'We've got almost enough to pay for the train fares for everyone, and some of the local shops have promised to give us things to make sandwiches and so on. You'll be going, Nellie, as a helper to look after the little ones.'

'Oh, really, Mum? But wouldn't you like to go?'

'No, you'll enjoy it more than me. Besides, you haven't seen the sea yourself, have you? I went when I was a little girl so it's your turn now.' She was more excited than the children if possible, as the days went by. But there was a disaster looming.

The unrest among the miners was growing both nationally and internationally. Despite all best efforts to negotiate on May 3rd, a general strike was called.

'This is it then,' Enoch announced.

'There's to be a general strike *in defence of miners' wages and hours*. It's an official statement. You can forget all the nonsense you've been talking about trip to the seaside. Any money that's been raised will be needed to keep miner's families together. Now, I have to be off. There's a union meeting at the Miner's Hall. You'd all better brace yourselves for the long haul. This could go on for many months.'

He crashed out of the house and as soon as he'd gone, Lizzie and Ben started to wail. Their father's shouting had upset them and they'd gathered that the seaside treat was going to be cancelled.

Nellie and her mother tried to comfort the children and spoke anxiously about the possible outcome. At least the community worked together at times like this and many families were willing to share what little they had. The children were encouraged to play together in the street and games were organised.

The news spread that many other workers were striking in support. Crisis talks were taking place, not that the Vale family knew much about that.

Their main thoughts lay with managing without Enoch and Joe's pay and trying to stop the two little ones from crying themselves to sleep at their disappointment about the seaside trip. There were conflicting reports coming from those who read the newspapers. Some said the Government were giving in and meeting the demands of the strikers. Others said that the strike was growing.

Finally, a few days later on May 12th, there was an announcement that the strike was to be called off. It was a few more days before anything returned to a semblance of order.

'Does this mean we can still go to the seaside?' asked Lizzie.

'We'll have to wait and see, love. But maybe. Maybe it will be all right.'

A New Life For Nellie

The first Saturday in June began with a clear blue sky and bright sunshine. The children were up early, ready for the long-awaited trip to the seaside. Despite all their fears, it was to go ahead.

When they arrived at the station, there was quite a crowd on the platform. The noise was deafening as more than forty excited children yelled at each other about their plans for the day. Nellie stood to one side, not liking to join the main group of adults who were in charge.

A collection of baskets with picnic food inside were waiting beside them and several more bags contained bottles of pop, kindly donated by Mrs Parks and other local shopkeepers.

They all clambered aboard the train

and one of the adults went to each carriage to check that there was someone responsible in charge.

'Can we have our dinner yet?' asked Ben inevitably, when they had been travelling for about a quarter-of-an-hour.

It was a totally magical day. The sun shone the whole time. Once they had all got over their first glimpse of the blue sea, they relaxed and though Lizzie kept eyeing it in case it came to knock her down, they all ran around shrieking and yelling and having the time of their lives.

Nellie's little group built a big heap of sand with their bare hands and decorated it with shells and bits of seaweed. She used one of the sandwich wrappers to make a flag on top and they all cheered as Castle Vale was named the best thing on the beach.

It was almost dark by the time the train pulled back into the local station. A few parents stood waiting outside and collected their weary children as they came through the gate. Everyone agreed, it had been the best day ever.

'Even better than Christmas,' a tired little Ben announced.

'Come on then, let's get you home. But you're right, it's been the best day ever,' Nellie agreed. 'We have to say a big thank you to everyone who helped to organise it. And now I've got lots of ideas for some new paintings.'

The memory of blue sea and sky and golden sands was to stay in Nellie's mind for a long time. She was still looking for a permanent job, but without luck. She even met Vera one day outside the factory but though she was as friendly as ever, she told her there was no point trying to get her job back. Florence was even higher up the pecking order and was now regularly seen walking out with Mr Albert.

'Disgusting, I say. Him a married man with a family. But you know Florence.

Nellie walked back home again, feeling very low. As she reached the corner shop, Mrs Parks waved to her.

'Come here a minute. I've heard of a job that might suit you. It's regular hours at least and won't be quite so hard on you as that bakery and everything else you've been doing to make ends meet.'

'Really? Where is it?'

'Well, it's a sort of maid and cleaner's job at the Cobridge house. The factory owner's house. It's a big place, but I hear as they're good people. Only snag is, it's live-in. But with all found, you'd be able to send money home.'

Clutching the carefully written reference from Mrs Parks that she had kept safe all this time, Nellie set out early the next morning. She knocked at the door of a large house owned by the Cobridge family, ironically the family who owned the china factory. A maid in a black dress and small white apron answered the door. When she heard Nellie's request, she hurriedly directed her round the back. Embarrassed, Nellie went round the big house and found the rear entrance. She had never realised there was a difference. Not a good start and she would have to be careful not to make any mistakes in such a posh place.

It was not the lady of the house who interviewed her, but a middle-aged woman in a dark blue dress with a white collar, her hair scraped back into a tight bun. She was Mrs Wilkinson, the housekeeper and responsible for engaging staff. She asked a great many questions and seemed pleased with the answers she heard.

'Well, Emily Parks seems satisfied enough with your character.'

'Oh, you know Mrs Parks, do you? She didn't mention it.'

'Known her for years. Her word is good enough for me. You get three meals a day, share a room with the other two maids. Uniform is provided. You get two evenings and one full day a week off, but you'll miss out when there's a function here. And you can sleep at home on the night before your day off. You return here by six, in time to help serve dinner. And you must be in by ten o'clock on your evenings off. If you choose to go out, that is.'

'Thank you. Does that mean I've got the job?'

'One month's trial. You'll be permanent once you prove yourself satisfactory.'

'Thank you. That all sounds very acceptable.'

'Start on Monday. You can bring one small suitcase or bag with your private things but storage space is limited so bear in mind what I say.'

After listing her various responsibilities Mrs Wilkinson dismissed Nellie with a nod.

'Ethel will show you out. Be here at eight o'clock prompt on Monday morning.'

The same maid showed her out and smiled in a friendly way. 'They're all right here. Mrs W. is a bit of a tartar but she's always fair and as long as you do what you're told, she's all right. How old are you?' Ethel asked suddenly.

'I'm nearly nineteen. Why?'

'You only look about thirteen. Bit skinny, aren't you?'

'Bit personal, aren't you? Maybe regular good food will help me grow a bit.' Nellie smiled at the girl, not wanting to leave on a sour note.

Nan had mixed feeling when Nellie told her the news. 'Oh, love, we shall miss you something chronic. How will I manage in the winter? And Lizzie will be very upset. You know what store she lays on you.'

'I know all about that, but it's good money for such work and I shall be able to give most of it to you. And I can come round two evenings every week and all day once a week. Much better than most live-ins get.'

'Well, I hope they're good to you. After what went on in the factory, watch out for yourself. Didn't they ask about that business?'

'No. Seems Mrs Parks is a friend of Mrs Wilkinson, that's the housekeeper, so she took her word for my good character. I'd best pop round to say thanks to her. Mrs Parks, that is.'

'So, who is it, lives at the big house?'

'Mr and Mrs Cobridge and I think maybe Mr James lives there as well. I didn't ask. Then there's one other maid, Ethel, that I met and Mrs Wilkinson and a cook.'

'I see. And they need that many to look after them, do they?'

'I s'pose so.'

'And what do you have to do?'

'Cleaning and, well, I don't really know. I should have asked, I suppose. I was just so glad to be taken on.'

'They'll probably tell you. Train you up, like. I don't expect they sit round a kitchen table like we do. They'll have all manner of knives and forks and plates. I knew someone who worked at a big house and she used to say you'd never believe all the fancy ways they had. Anyway love, well done. I hope it all works out. Come here. Give me a cuddle.'

'Thanks, Mum. I think it going to be

the start of something really new. A whole change in my life. I shall miss the painting though. I loved doing that best of all. And Vera and the girls. It was always such fun in the workshop, even if it was quite hard work.'

It was quite a strange weekend. Nellie was pausing every few minutes, looking around her home and the family as if was making she sure she would remember every detail.

★   ★   ★

She spent extra time with Lizzie and Ben, telling them stories and playing games, feeling that things would never be the same again.

'I don't want you to go away, Nellie,' wailed Lizzie as she went to bed on Sunday night. 'It's not the same when you're not here.'

'I'll be back soon. You'll scarce notice I've gone.'

But her sister continued to cry for a long time and Nellie felt her own eyes stinging with tears.

It was indeed, the start of a whole new way of life. At seven-thirty on Monday, Nellie left home with a few possessions in a shopping bag. She was unsure about what she would need to take but she would be home again soon and could collect anything else she might need and it was only a short walk.

She had put in a change of underclothes, her favourite book and a small notepad. They had said a uniform was provided so she expected she would wear that most of the time. There might not be much time for reading or anything else, when she finished work so she kept everything to a minimum.

It was early when she reached Cobridge House, but she was used to being at work much earlier in the factory and this seemed a very easy start. She went to the back door and knocked timidly. Ethel let her in and took her straight to the room they would share. A plain grey dress hung on a hook behind the door and a black dress on another hanger. A whitecap and apron were folded on the top of a small chest of drawers.

'This is the one you wear in the morning and before lunch,' Ethel said picking up the grey dress. 'You change into the black if you have to serve lunch. Sometimes, when just the mistress is home, she has lunch on a tray in the breakfast room and we don't have to change to serve her then.'

'I hope someone will explain to me how we wait at the table. I haven't ever done anything like that.'

'Don't worry. Mrs Wilkinson will put you through your paces before she'll let you loose on the mistress. We usually share the waiting on and you'll probably start with the tea. That's easy. She likes to pour herself and you just have to hand it round to any guests. The mistress is very nice really. Straight, if you know what I mean. Doesn't stand any nonsense but she's fair. More than I can say of some of their snooty guests when they come. Anyway, you'll be introduced later on this morning.'

'I thought I was just going to be a cleaner.'

'We have two women who come in to do the heavy work. Carpets and moving the furniture to do the floors behind it and such like. We do the dusting every day and polishing once a week. The rest is table laying, waiting on and some-times, when there's a big do on, we help polish silver and set out the special things.'

It seemed there were a lot of people to look after such a small family. She had learned there were no young children, just Mr and Mrs Cobridge and their son, James.

'Mr James is nice, isn't he?'

Ethel stared at her. 'How do you know? Any road up, don't let anyone hear you saying things like that. Especially not Mrs W. She'll have your guts for garters. Mr James is right out of reach. He wouldn't even notice us if he fell over us in the passage. Anyway, how do you know if he's nice or ugly as sin?'

'I met him at the factory once. I used to work there.'

'Get the sack, did you?'

'Well, yes. But it wasn't my fault. I was accused of something I didn't do. Anyways, here I am, ready to do whatever I have to do.'

'You'd best start by putting on your uniform. Looking at you and the size of the dress, I reckon we'll need some pins to stop it droppin' off you. The last girl must have been twice your size.'

Nellie took off her own dress and pulled the grey one over her head. It practically reached the floor. There was a belt to go with it so she hitched it up and made a sort of fold over. At least she could walk without tripping up now but the outfit was clearly very much too large.

'Hmm. Maybe they'll fatten you up till you fit it,' Ethel said with a grin. They both burst out laughing and only managed to get their faces straight when they heard Mrs Wilkinson coming up the back stairs.

'Good girl. I see you've got yourself changed. Oh dear, that's not very satisfactory, is it?'

'I'm sorry. I've sort of pulled it up with the belt, but it's big everywhere.'

'Maisie comes in to do some sewing on Thursday. Perhaps she can take it in a bit. Mind you, it may need more than a bit. We might have to see the mistress and consider if she might order a new dress for you. Well, two, I suppose. Oh, dearie me. Not a good start.'

Nellie looked down and mumbled that she was sorry, but the housekeeper waved away her words. The rest of the morning was spent learning how to dust. It was much more than pushing some old rag over the furniture and she even had to learn that the soft yellow duster was held in a particular way. She was given her instructions.

'You need to gather the dust inside it, not wipe it off the tops and drop it onto the floor. When you finish dusting the room, you take the duster outside the back door and give it a good shake, ready to start the next room. At the end of the morning, it goes into the washing basket in the scullery. Is that all clear?'

'Yes, Mrs Wilkinson.'

'Good. You can get on with it now. Oh and if you see any of the family, stand aside and look away. Never speak to them unless they speak to you first, understand?' Nellie nodded though she didn't really agree with what she was being told. They were all just people, after all. The Cobridges were just fortunate to be rich and probably no better than her own family. But she held her tongue.

No need to upset anyone before she even started. She began working in the imposing entrance hall. The walls were panelled in dark oak and several large chests stood around. Carefully, she dusted the elaborate carving and wondered what was kept inside them. A large decorated vase stood on a side table. It was beautifully painted and she let her fingers run over the delicate work. She heard a door open behind her and quickly dusted the surface of the vase in case she had left a finger-mark. Mrs Wilkinson stood behind her watching as she worked.

'Good girl,' she said approvingly as she passed into one of the other rooms. She stopped at the doorway and called her over. 'You'd better take a look in the other rooms. The mistress isn't here yet so you can come and see what needs to be done.'

The magnificent drawing room was possibly the biggest room Nellie had even seen in a private home. The walls were papered in a pretty floral design and there were comfy-looking sofas and armchairs grouped around the room.

The carpet was deep red and very luxurious, though Nellie noticed several odd threads were lying on it. There was a large china cabinet running almost the entire length of one wall. It was filled with collections of china showing every pattern she had seen in the factory and a whole lot more. Even her old familiar rose tea set was there and a number of magnificent large vases, similar to the one on the hall.

'Oh, aren't they wonderful?' Nellie breathed. 'They must have one of everything the factory ever made.'

'You can look, but don't touch. Some of these are very precious.'

'Don't they ever get dusted?' she asked longingly. 'I'd just love to be able to touch them sometimes.'

'Once a month we have a specialist cleaning lady comes in to dust them. She works around the big pottery owners' homes and in the showrooms of several places. She knows how to handle it and how best to clean it.'

'P'raps if she comes on one of my days off, I can stay and watch her?'

'Don't be silly, child. It's only china. You'll get your fill of touching it when you help with the washing up after one of the big dinner parties. Now, I'll show you some of the other rooms while it's quiet. Oh dear, we really shall have to do something about that uniform,' she remarked as Nellie tucked the long skirt back into the belt.

Mrs Wilkinson showed her room after room. 'Now Nellie, as you can see, this is the dining room. Ethel will show you the routine in here. Now, I'd better go and speak to Cook. You'll have your lunch at noon. The family eat at one o'clock when they are home. Ethel will show you where we eat.'

The two girls worked quietly together and dusted every inch of the room and furniture. To Nellie, it looked clean to start with but she said nothing and continued to wipe her cloth over every corner. The door opened and the man she recognised as Mr Cobridge came in.

'Mornin', girls,' he said briskly. 'Left a folder of papers somewhere. Have you seen them?'

'No, Sir,' Ethel said with almost a curtsey. 'Not in here, anyways.'

'Damnation. Where have I put it?' He

swept out again and shut the door noisily.

'That's the Master, Mr Cobridge.'

'Yes, I know. I saw him when I worked at the factory.'

'He didn't know you then.'

'Course not. There are dozens of people work there. Now, what's next? I suppose we have to go and shake the imaginary dust out of our dusters.'

Ethel giggled. 'Might be all right working with you. You've got a bit of a spark, haven't you?'

'I'm not sure what you mean, but I hope we'll get on all right. By the way, who's the other girl who shares our room? There are three beds in there.'

'That's Clara. Her mum's been taken bad so she's had a few days off. You turned up in the nick of time or I'd have been doing the work of three.'

'It's not exactly hard work, though, is it?' Nellie remembered the long hard days she spent at the bakery, not to mention the days before she had become a paintress.

'You've seen nothing yet. Just you wait till there's guests staying or one of the dinner parties. You'll be glad of days when it's a bit lighter.'

'So, what's Clara like?'

'Bit moody. Can't really have a laugh with her, but I s'pose she's had it tough. Her dad died in the war and her mum's on her own most of the time. She hasn't got brothers or sisters. What about you? Have you got any brothers and sisters?'

Nellie told her new friend about her family and recounted tales of the magical day they'd spent at the seaside. The clock struck in the hall.

'Cripes, we'd better get a move on, Old Ma W. will be after us. Quick whip round the drawing room and we can say we've done it. Go quietly so she doesn't realise we've only just gone in there.'

A few minutes later, they went back to the kitchen and what Nellie learned was the servants' dining room. It was a cosy room with a large scrubbed table in the middle and seats round it with room for everyone.

'Right, girls, you lay up for your lunches. Six of us today. You can go and change after we've eaten, Master and Mistress are both in for lunch. Nellie, you can carry the dishes up and Ethel will serve. Watch carefully what she does and then I'll show you properly afterwards so you can take your turn. Clara will be back tomorrow, by the way, so you can have your day off on Wednesday, Ethel. You'll have Friday this week, Nellie.'

'Thanks, Mrs Wilkinson,' Ethel replied.

'Yes, thank you,' Nellie added, as it seemed to be expected.

'I'll introduce you to Mrs Cobridge after lunch, so mind you're to be polite and keep your eyes lowered until spoken to. You call her Ma'am when she speaks to you. Don't look so worried. She's a very nice lady and apart from the uniform that's several sizes too large, she won't find fault with you, I'm sure.'

★ ★ ★

'If this is a sample of the food here, I think I'm going to be very happy,' Nellie said after clearing her plate. It was a very tasty shepherd's pie today, followed by rice pudding.

She felt so full after eating the unusually large meal, she was ready for a sleep. But, it was straight upstairs to their room to change into the black uniform and white apron. Ethel helped her to pin the cap in place over her soft hair.

They scuttled down the servants' stairs and into the kitchen. The dishes were ready and waiting to be carried through. A gong sounded and they heard the dining room doors opening. Nellie was extremely nervous as it all sounded so very much beyond her experience. But she needn't have worried. It was all very smooth and she

101

passed things to Ethel and removed them when necessary. She caught on very quickly. Just as she thought her first ordeal was over, Mrs Cobridge spoke to her.

'Come here, dear,' she said. Nellie was so surprised at being called dear. She looked around to see if it was someone else being spoken to like that. 'You must be the new girl. Nellie, isn't it?'

'Yes, Mrs . . . er, Ma'am. Nellie Vale.'

'Welcome, Nellie. I hope you'll be happy here. Oh dear, I think we shall have to get Mrs Wilkinson to do something about your uniform. That won't do at all. Ask her to come and see me this afternoon.'

'Yes, Ma'am.'

'That will be all for now. I look forward to getting to know you in good time.'

'Yes, Ma'am. Thank you, Ma'am.' She practically curtsied as she left the room.

Mr and Mrs Cobridge looked at each

other and began to laugh.

'Looks like the Dragon Lady put the fear of God into her. Poor kid. Something familiar about her though. Has she been here before?'

'Not that I know of. Where might you have seen her?'

'I've no idea. They all look the same, don't they? Now, I'd better get myself down to the factory. Few things to sort out and James was asking for my advice about something. I'll be out for dinner this evening. I have a meeting.'

'Oh, how disappointing. You know how I hate dining alone.'

'James will be in, I don't doubt. Have a nice afternoon.'

A knock sounded and Mrs Wilkinson came in.

'Ah, good. Please will you sort out proper clothing for the poor child who's joined the staff? Our usual supplier should have something ready made. Send her down this afternoon. I can't have her dressed like that. Nice little thing. I hope she works out.'

'Thank you, Mrs Cobridge. I'll see to it right away. I think she will be satisfactory. She seems a bright girl and willing to work. Typical of the girls of the area. One of a large family. Miners they are. Suffering the same way most of them are in the present difficult times.'

When she told Nellie the news about her new uniform, she was delighted.

'I've never been to a shop before to have a ready-made dress. My mum usually makes things for me and I help her. Just think, two new dresses, ready-made for me.'

'It's only a uniform, girl. Nothing you can wear except here at work. If it pleases you so much, you can buy something for yourself when you get your wages.'

'Oh no, I couldn't do that. I promised my mum that I'd take my earnings home. She really needs it for the family. We're always afraid Dad's going to be laid off. He had an injury, you know, and it's only cos my brother works alongside him that he's kept on. So you see, I get my keep here and clothes so I can send all my wages home.'

'You're a mug then, Nellie,' Ethel chimed in. 'You should keep a bit back for yourself. Have you told them how much you earn?'

Nellie shook her head.

'If you haven't, you can always say you earned a bit less and then you can save up.'

'Less of the tittle tattle and a bit more work. Nellie, you go and change into your outdoor things and get down the Wright's store. I'll give you a note to put on the mistress's account. One black and one grey dress. No, wait, we'll get two of the grey so one can be in the wash.'

Wright's usually kept maids' dresses ready-made in several sizes. Employers were rarely willing to wait for uniforms to be made specially. When Nellie arrived, they had only one grey dress and the black one was slightly too large.

The assistant was apologetic.

'I can get it altered for you by tomorrow and another grey one by early next week. I'm sorry, but you're rather smaller than we usually fit.'

'I see,' Nellie said. 'I'm not sure if they'll let me come back tomorrow.' She felt disappointed.

'Well, seeing as it's Mrs Cobridge, I'll get it delivered to the house.'

'Thanks very much. I'm sure that will be a help.'

Clutching her parcel, neatly wrapped in brown paper and tied with string, she went back to her new home. She had the feeling that life was looking up and gave a little skip as she walked along the uneven pavement. Even the Potteries smell wasn't so bad up here on the hill, where the nobs lived.

Master James Shows An Interest

Nellie knocked at the back door when she arrived at the house. The door was always locked so there was never any chance of going in or out without someone knowing. Mrs Wilkinson told her to go and change into the large dress for now. Then she was to help lay for dinner for two. Ethel would tell her what cutlery to use and how it was set.

'Then I shall come and inspect it. Get along with you.'

Just as they were finishing, the door opened and Mr James came in. Ethel bobbed towards him.

'Sorry, Sir. We'll come back later.'

'No, carry on. I just wanted to look at something. You won't be in my way. Don't I know you?' he asked Nellie.

'Not really, Sir. But you have seen

me. I used to work in the decorating shop at the factory.'

'Yes, of course I remember you. With Vera and her bench.' Nellie was surprised. She looked into his clear blue eyes. He was so good-looking with neat fair hair and a ready smile.

'Well, yes, that's right. Only I was sacked.'

'Oh, dear,' he said with a slight smile. 'What did you do? Pinch someone's tea mug?'

'I didn't do anything, Sir. I was accused but I didn't do it.'

Ethel was nudging her. The girl was forgetting her place and Mrs W. would be on the warpath, not that she'd tell tales on her, but it was pushing things a bit.

'Sorry, Sir, I have to get on with my work now.'

James said no more and watched as she went out. He did remember her clearly. Vera had mentioned that she had natural talent as a paintress and was pleased with her progress in a short time. Natural talent needed to be nurtured, James always believed. He would take a personal interest in this little maid, he decided.

When Clara came back, there was more of a black air descended on the little working group. She was a large girl who rarely smiled and grumbled a great deal. Perhaps she was worried about her mother, Nellie decided, and tried to give her a friendly smile whenever they passed each other during the day.

By Thursday evening, Nellie was packed and ready to go home as soon as dinner was over. She was allowed to stay for the night and arrived home when everyone except her mother was already in bed.

'I'll tell you all about it tomorrow. I'm worn out now. Night, Mum. It's nice to be back.' She went up the stairs and crept into bed beside Lizzie. The little girl snuggled up to her sister as if she'd never been away. Well, it was only four days after all.

When the men had gone to work and

Ben to school, the three females sat sipping tea. Lizzie was hanging on to her beloved sister's skirt while Nan listened with great interest to everything her daughter had to say.

'And you should see the china, Mum. It's so lovely. I could just keep touching it to see if it's real.'

'You always did like nice china, didn't you. Play your cards right and maybe Mr James will give you another chance.'

'I don't think so. I'll never get back in there as long as Albert is manager along with his little pet. Still I'm happy enough, so far. We get lovely food and regular hours. Mind you, there hasn't been a big dinner party yet. I think there's one tomorrow so maybe I'll change my mind after that.'

The day passed all too quickly and it was time to say goodbye. Lizzie was less unhappy this time, knowing she would see her sister again soon.

'I won't know which day I get off next week. But Wednesday night I'm getting the evening off anyway, so I can pop round to see you anyway to let you know. Then I can see Dad and Joe for a bit as well. It's only half-an-hour's walk. Must go now.'

Nan felt reassured. The girl was making a go if it and seemed happy enough.

The dinner party on Saturday night showed how things really were at a busy time. Ethel and Clara did the waiting at table, with Nellie acting as runner between the dining room and kitchen. Mrs Wilkinson had trays ready in the kitchen as Cook completed the dishes. They had an extra girl brought in to wash the pots as they were used and finished.

'With all this show of grandeur, they ought to have a butler,' Mrs Wilkinson grumbled. 'Not that anyone has a butler in this area. Now when I worked in London . . . ' She often mentioned this but they were all too busy to listen on this occasion.

It was eleven o'clock before the party broke up. The three girls were exhausted and there was still a great deal of clearing to be done. Most of the dirty dishes had been removed from the dining room but there were still a number of things on the table to be put away. Washing up was barely halfway through so it looked like being an extremely late night before they could go to bed. Nellie was sent to put away some of the china ornaments, largely because Mrs Wilkinson had seen the girl's delight in the beautiful objects, but mostly because she treated them with almost a reverential care.

'You still working?' Mr James remarked as he came into the dining room. 'You must be exhausted. On the go since early morning.' He watched as she carefully wiped the precious items and moved them to their correct places. 'You really love this china, don't you?'

'Course I do. Sorry, I mean, yes, Sir.'

'Mrs Wilkinson been giving you instructions on how to address us royalty, has she?'

'Yes, Sir. We mustn't look straight at

you or speak unless spoken to.'

'Well, you can forget about that when you're speaking to me. In private of course. I don't want to get you into trouble with the Dragon Lady.'

'Dragon Lady?' Nellie giggled.

'Oh, yes. That's what we call her. We have rules too, you know. We mustn't speak in a familiar way to any of you. Mustn't give you any ideas above your station. So tell me, why are you so keen on fine china?'

'I loved handling it at the factory. It was the best time of my life when I was made up to a full paintress.'

'Shame you had to leave. Do you want to tell me about it?'

'Better not. I'd best get back to the kitchen now or the Dragon Lady will be after me.' Nellie giggled again. She could hardly wait to tell Ethel what Mr James had said.

'I'd like to talk with you some more. Will you spend some time with me on your night off?'

'Oh, but I couldn't, Sir. What would

everyone think?'

'What do you do on your night off? Do you have a gentleman friend?'

'What, me? Course not. I'm going home on my next night off on Wednesday. I shall have to go as they'll be expecting me.'

'Tell me where home is and I'll meet you and walk you back.'

Nellie blushed. She didn't want him to see their house. He'd really know what a poor little thing she was and he'd never want to talk to her, not ever again. Besides, it wouldn't do to walk anywhere with him and in any case, Joe or her father would probably accompany her back as it was so late at night.

'I couldn't, Sir. Really, I couldn't. I have to go now.'

James gave a shrug and stood aside for her to pass.

'I won't give up on you. You're a talented girl, I remember. Much too bright to be one of our maids. Tell you what. You have a bit of time off in the afternoons, don't you?'

Nellie nodded. 'Right, then I want you to look at some books. Pottery illustrations and some of the technical books about manufacture. I'll leave them out for you. What do you say?'

'Oh, how lovely. I'd like that. But you'd have to explain to Mrs W. I don't want her thinking I've stolen them or anything.'

'Don't worry. I'll tell her it's a task for me. Research. I don't suppose you'll understand all of it but you'll like the pictures. Oh, sorry, I suppose you can read, can't you? Of course you can,' he added seeing her face flicker with anger. 'And I'll get you to do some drawing and painting for me. Designs. I suspect you can come up with some new ideas.'

'Oh, Sir, I'd really love that, but I don't know when I'll find time to do any of it. I'm kept very busy here.'

'We'll sort something out. Now go on with you. Good night.'

Nellie floated her way down to the kitchen. Mr James had taken a real interest in her. He liked her, she was certain of it. And he thought she might have talent. Maybe, just maybe, one day she might get back to painting beautiful china.

'Where on earth have you been till now?' Mrs Wilkinson demanded.

'Sorry, but Mr James started talking to me. I said I had to get back but he kept asking me stuff about the china. He remembered I used to work at the factory.'

'That's as may be, but now you work here. No slacking off, talking to your betters. Whatever must they think of you? Do you understand?'

'Yes.'

'Now, get off to bed. And don't be late in the morning. And Nellie . . . you did well tonight.'

'Thank you. Good night.' *Dragon Lady* she whispered to herself with a giggle.

Despite feeling exhausted, she couldn't fall asleep. She felt a sense of something coming her way soon. The start of a new phase in her life, just as she'd said to her mother last week. Was it really only last week? This time last week she hadn't even begun to work here and yet already she felt it had been a lifetime.

'Stop tossing and turning, Nellie,' grumbled Ethel. You're keeping us all awake.'

'Sorry. I'll try to keep still.' Creaking iron bedsteads and comfort didn't go together, but Nellie did her best to ignore the bits that seemed to be sticking into her at all angles.

True to his word, Mr James had left a pile of books in the small room they called a library. He left a note on top saying they were for Nellie to look at and please do not replace them on the shelves until he asked.

'What do you want with books?' Clara demanded.

'I was talking about the china they make and Mr James thought I'd like to look at some of the pictures.'

'I s'pose he thinks you can read them, does he?'

'Well, yes, I can read. Can't you?'

'Course I can. Well, a bit. Couldn't get to school all that much. Had me ma to look after, didn't I?'

'I'm sorry.' Though books had never been a priority in Nellie's house, she had always managed to find some way of reading. She had read everything in the school's little library and some of her teachers had lent her books. She had two of her own, won as prizes for neat handwriting and good behaviour at school. She knew just about every word of them by heart. Evidently Clara had never had the same chances.

When she took her hour off after lunch, Nellie went into the library and turned the pages of the richly illustrated books. Even the smell of the pristine pages was a pleasure to the girl and she touched the glossy pictures as if she was caressing the china itself.

She was soon engrossed in the words as well, learning something of the history of china and more about the manufacturing process. All too soon, her time ran out and the clock on the mantelpiece chimed the hour. She gave a start and closed the books carefully and went to the kitchen to begin serving tea.

Mrs Wilkinson was unhappy at this latest development. It interfered with her discipline of the staff. Favouritism like that would be unpopular with the others. She might need to have a word with the mistress. It just wasn't right for servants to be allowed access to any of the family's rooms.

'Well, if the child is interested, I can't see it does any harm. After all, it's thanks to the company that any of us are here. I'll have a word with Mr James. See if I can find out why he is taking such an interest in this maid. Thank you for bringing it to my attention.'

Mrs Cobridge dismissed her housekeeper and returned to her journal. She frowned. In truth, it wasn't good to single out one of the maids this way, but she wasn't going to allow anyone to criticise her son. She might do it herself but nobody else could.

Whenever he could, James sought out Nellie and talked about their shared passion for beautiful china.

'You should come down to the factory sometime and look at our little museum. It isn't really a museum, just a collection of all the pieces we have made. More than we have here. You know my great-grandfather started the factory? It's come on a long way since those days. We're starting to improve on automation now. And health regulations are much better than they were.'

Nellie listened to him, totally captivated not only by the subject but also by the man himself. She had never met anyone like him before. He was one of the bosses in his factory but he was spending time with her, just a maid in the family home. She was a nobody and dressed in an ugly maid's outfit but he looked at her as if she was somebody important in her own right.

'I can't come to the factory. What

would they think of me? I couldn't be seen anywhere in that place. It might get back to Mr Albert and the girls.'

'Oh, tish. You're much too concerned about what people think.'

'Well, it matters to me. It's all right for you. You're an important man. You have money and a beautiful home. I rely on your family to give me my keep and wages. My family haven't got anything and they rely on my wages just to scrape a living.'

'I'm sorry, Nellie. I don't mean to criticise but if it wasn't for people like you and the girls, as you call them, we wouldn't have any of this. No lovely home. No money. No servants. Don't ever undervalue yourself.

'I want to get you back where you should be. Using your God-given talents. Now, I've got a decent pad of paper for you to do some designs. I expect you prefer to use watercolours so I've brought a box of them home. You can use the little office next to my room. Do the work whenever you have spare time and leave it out to dry. I rarely use the room, so you won't be disturbed or be in my way. Just paint whatever comes into your head but bear in mind the shapes of cups and plates that might use the design.'

She listened to his words and a shiver of excitement rushed through her body. If she produced something he liked, she might even get back to painting, though how she could ever fit into the decorating shop again, she couldn't think.

'I can try. I'd like that but I can't promise anything. I might not be good enough.'

'Have you seen some of the new art deco designs? Have a look in the shops. It's early days yet but I think this is going to be big. I'll bring some pictures home so you see what I'm talking about.'

'I'm sorry, Sir, but I don't know what you're talking about. Art what? I haven't heard of it. I'm only a maid, Sir. Please don't give me ideas above my station. As for looking in shops, when have I got time for anything like that?'

'If you're going to be a designer, you need to know what's going on.'

'A designer? Me? You've hardly seen anything I can do. Why me? I've only been a paintress for a short time and then only one in a line of people working on one bench in the factory. I'm nobody special. Just forget about me and stop trying to give me ideas. Mrs Wilkinson . . . '

'Forget the Dragon Lady. Do this for me. I've seen how you look at china. How sensitively you touch it. You get a look in your eye that suggests to me that you can do more. So much more than dusting.'

Nellie felt near to tears. She knew that what he was saying was right. She did love the china. She did indeed think she might be able to paint quite well, but it was all a dream. She had cleaning to do. She had to wait at table. That was her role in life.

'I've got to go. I'll be in trouble if I'm not there to help the others. Thank you for taking an interest but I'm a just maid with work to do.' She fled from the room and went to her shared bedroom to wipe the tears of frustration from her eyes.

'Been talking to Mr James again, have you,' Clara said with an edge to her voice that conveyed sharp criticism.

'There's something he wanted me to do,' Nellie said, reverting to a strong Potteries accent she had been trying to put behind her. It wouldn't do if the others thought she was trying to show them up.

'Quite the young master's little favourite these days, aren't you? Just take care. Chances are he wants something more than a chat.'

'Don't be disgusting. Mr James is a gentleman.'

'Yes, but he's a man as well. Men only want one thing from a maid. Mark my words. You want to watch him. Don't let yourself be on your own with him too much. Wandering hands and all that.'

'Oh, for goodness sake, Ethel, Clara. What would he want with a skinny little thing like me? He's got the pick of every good looking woman for miles around. You saw how that Miss Salisbury looked at him at that dinner the other night. And she's the daughter of one of the big company owners. Beautiful with it.'

The two other maids sighed. Nellie was a nice enough girl and a hard worker, but she was just too innocent for her own good.

'Just watch yourself, is all I'm saying. Men can have a whole tribe of beautiful women parading in front of them but believe me, they always want a bit on the side if they can get it.'

'Best get down to the kitchen. See what Mrs W. has got lined up for us.'

'The Dragon Lady, Mr James calls her.'

'No. Really? But they're the bosses.' The girls began giggling and laughed till tears ran down their faces.

'Oh, Nellie, you're a caution right enough. Maybe having someone knowing the bosses might be worthwhile after all. I doubt I shall ever be able to keep a straight face again when she rants at me,' Ethel spluttered.

'She'll be ranting right enough if we don't get down right away.' The three girls went down the wooden stairs, clattering in their haste to get there on time.

'You're very noisy today. The mistress will be complaining, I don't doubt. Now, Ethel, you take the tea in. The mistress is in the drawing room with one guest. Nellie, you go and open the door, please. And get the table out ready. Hurry now, she rang several minutes ago. Come straight back, Nellie. I have a task for you.'

Word had obviously got back to Mrs Wilkinson about her liaison with Mr James. She kept the girl working extremely hard for most of the next two days. There was no time for painting, even if she'd had a mind to do it.

Her evening off had been curtailed to a mere hour-and-a-half so she had only a short time to be with her family. She told her mother about Mr James and his interest in her. Her mother was very concerned and gave her the same warnings as the other maids.

'But Mr James is a real gentleman, Mum. He'd never take advantage of me. I just know he wouldn't.'

'All the same, take care and don't let yourself be alone with him. Now, our Joe, I want you to walk Nellie back to Cobridge House.'

She linked arms with her younger brother. He was taller than she was now and she could feel his muscles had grown stronger.

'You've become quite a man these days. How's it going?'

'Oh, you know. Same as ever. Dad's not much better. I don't know he keeps it a secret, you know, his bad arm. It's still giving him a lot of pain but he uses his other arm a bit and I keep doing the rest. But honest, Nellie, I hate it down there. There's nowt else I can do, though. I have to keep at it for our Dad and for the others. Money's not so tight now and when your wage starts coming in, we'll be better still. What did you think of our Mum?'

'She looks all right. Why?'

'She's coughing a lot again. I'm afraid she's starting to be bad again. And you're not here to look after her this winter.'

They were reaching Cobridge House before the conversation had really finished.

'Keep a lookout for her, won't you? I'm not sure when I'll be home again. Things are busier than ever here, but I'll see you soon. Bye love. It's nice to have a big brother now.'

'Bye, Nellie. Tek care o' thee sen.'

'Ah reet lad,' she laughed. She had almost been forgetting her dialect lately. Wouldn't do to seem like someone she wasn't. She ran round to the back of the house and heard the church clock strike ten. She raised her hand to knock when she heard someone behind her. She knocked loudly at the door, hoping it would be opened quickly.

'It's all right, Nellie. It's only me.'

'Mr James? What are you doing at the back door?'

'I was waiting for you. I think you've been avoiding me, haven't you?'

'Not really, Sir. There's been a lot of work on lately.'

'And your gentleman friend? Who was that? I thought you told me you weren't walking out with anyone.'

'Walking out? That was me brother, Sir. He walked me back so I wasn't out on my own.'

James laughed.

'Oh, I see. He's a big lad. Older than you is he?'

'No, Sir. He's five years younger. I am a bit of a shrimp, aren't I?' The light went on in the passageway. 'You'd better go now, Sir. I don't want them seeing you with me.'

'Oh, dear, still giving you trouble are they?'

'Go away,' she hissed.

'You're late,' Mrs Wilkinson snapped.

'I did knock, but you mustn't have heard me,' Nellie protested.

'Is there someone with you?' the housekeeper asked, peering past Nellie into the dark passageway.

'No, I'm all alone.' She kept her fingers crossed that Mr James wasn't spotted. It wouldn't do her reputation any good at all.

Nellie Is Forced Out

Whenever she could find a few minutes, Nellie went to the little room to paint. She could get lost in her work if she wasn't careful and be late for her duties. She let her imagination run wild and painted bold designs in bright colours.

James took to leaving notes for her. He told her the designs he liked and those he didn't. He suggested that some of her design shapes would be impossible to manufacture.

She left him notes to say she didn't have enough time to spare and that she was always scared of being late. He put a little bedside clock near the desk so that she was always able to see exactly what time it was. They hadn't actually spoken for several days, but when she

131

was serving dinner, a skill she now had learned to Mrs Wilkinson's satisfaction, he always tried to wink at her and saved his special smile just for her when she put down his plate. One evening, he cornered her in the dining room as the table was being cleared.

'I am most impressed by your paintings, Nellie. They are great, just what I wanted. You have a raw talent, but talent it certainly is. The potential is there. You need to improve on your techniques a little, but I think we need to look at making you part of our design team. What do you say?'

'Your design team? What do you mean? Be a proper artist sort of thing? But you said I need to improve my techny . . . something. How can I do that?'

'Don't worry about it. I'll take care of that. I'll have a word with my father.'

'But Sir, I need my wages from here. And I'd have to live at home again. I like living here. I know I have work to do, but I get paid and if I'm at home,

I'll have to do all the chores again and . . . and . . . '

'Shut up, girl.' He put a finger on her lips to stop her talking. She felt her heart beat a little faster at his touch. She pulled away. This was exactly what they'd all warned her would happen. He wanted her for something else and she didn't really know what, except it was something bad.

'It's all right, Nellie. I'm not going to harm you. Just the opposite. I like you. I like you a lot. You've got talent and I want to see it grow. You're much too bright to waste your life cleaning and waiting at a table. Don't worry about a thing. I shall speak to my father and see what we can do for you. Meanwhile, carry on with your painting. I'll put some larger sheets of paper in my office.'

★ ★ ★

Nellie neither saw nor heard anything of Mr James for the next few days.

There were no encouraging little notes left for her. She asked the others if they knew anything, but they said nothing.

A week later, he was back. Nellie felt her heart give a little leap when he came into the hallway carrying a suitcase.

'Hello, Nellie. Hope you've got lots of designs for me to see. Can you manage my bag? It's not too heavy. Take it up to my room, if you would. I need to see Mother. Is she in the drawing room?'

'Yes, Sir. She's just taking tea.'

'Jolly good. I'm dying of thirst.' He breezed in to see his mother. Nellie watched as the door closed. Was he going to say something about her to his mother?

She picked up his suitcase and took it up to his room. She lingered for a moment, looking at the dark furniture and the old gold bedcover.

Very manly, she thought, especially after the light floral things in the mistress's room.

'What were you doing in there, girl?' Mrs Wilkinson demanded as Nellie was coming from Mr James's room.

'Nothing, Mrs Wilkinson. I was just taking up the young master's suitcase, like he asked me to.'

'Very well. Get down to the drawing room. Tea is finished and they want the tray clearing.'

Nellie ran down the stairs and knocked at the door. 'Mrs Wilkinson says you've finished with the tea things and I'm to clear them away.'

'Yes, Nellie. Thank you. James tells me you have been doing some drawings for him. I should like to see them. Bring them to me when you have cleared tea.'

'Oh, well, yes, Ma'am. But they're not very good. I mean, I don't have any techni . . . something. Everyone says so. And I haven't got time to go and get any.'

Mrs Cobridge stifled a smile. 'Bring them anyway. I'd still like to see them, with or without techni something.'

Nellie cleared the cups and plates on

to the tray and lifted it. James opened the door for her and gave her an encouraging smile.

She put the tray down on the kitchen table and left the others to wash up, calling that the mistress needed her to do something as she ran up the back stairs to the little room.

She bundled the paintings together and took them down, this time using the front stairs so the others didn't see what she was carrying. She knocked on the door and went inside. Nervously, she handed the pile of papers to Mrs Cobridge and stood back, waiting for a comment.

'Yes, some of these are very good. I'm not sure about these rather brash colours, though.'

'But Mother, this is the up and coming thing. They are not popular yet but believe me, they will be. It's all about shape and a complete break with tradition.'

'I think it's too risky. Your father will never agree to any of this. I quite like the all-over pastel flower designs. Your children's things are also delightful. Where did you get the inspiration for them?'

'I used to tell stories to my little sister. I thought of them when I was drawing these. Thank you, Ma'am.'

'You may go now, Nellie. I'm sure you have duties to attend to.'

'Thank you, Ma'am.' She bobbed a token curtsey, feeling it was necessary.

'I wish she wouldn't do that, Mother. Can't you tell the Dragon Lady to stop them curtseying?'

'She wouldn't listen. Oh, I don't mind. At least it proves they know their place. The designs are very interesting, but I'm not sure your father will allow her to go and work at the factory. You said she was dismissed? Not a good sign. Expect she stole something or made herself unpopular in some way.'

'I'm not letting it rest. I think she's worth more than being a maid.'

'James? You're not keen on this girl for some other reason are you? You haven't been . . . ' she couldn't bring herself to actually voice her suspicions.

'Of course not, Mother. What do you take me for? I admit, I am fond of the little thing. She's had a tough life and I want to help her to better herself.'

'Just keep your distance from her. I don't want any unhealthy liaisons in this house. Do you understand? I'm not having a son of mine taking up with some little housemaid. Gracious, what on earth would people think?'

'You know, Mother, I don't care what people think. I really care about Nellie and people like her. It's time we started to realise that all God's people are equal.'

'Don't be ridiculous, James. I don't know what's come over you. Your father will be furious at your suggestions. As for Nellie, you can forget all about her. It's as if you're trying to make her think she's as good as we are. I cannot believe it after all the advantages you've been given. Now I must go and rest before dinner. I feel quite faint.' She left the room in a cloud of expensive perfume while James ground his teeth together.

Whatever his mother said, he knew she was breaking new ground in design. He thought of his mother's words. Unhealthy liaisons? Taking up with a housemaid? Snobbishness entirely. He liked the housemaid in question. There was nothing unhealthy about their liaison, if such it could be called. It was all very innocent.

Maybe it was time to take her out with him and see just how much she could cope with a betterment of life. He decided to invite her out for dinner the very next time she had an evening off. He knew better than to say anything to anyone else and would look for an opportunity to ask her privately. But would she agree?

Mrs Cobridge was troubled. In her well-ordered, unchallenging life, she was potentially facing the worst situation she had ever dealt with. Knowing how stubborn her son could be, she had to think carefully.

James had been away on a business trip for the company. She needed to make certain he went away again and resolved to ask her husband to invent some good reason for him to make another trip, a longer one this time. While he was away, she would find some reason to dismiss the wretched girl.

It was a pity, as Nellie had proved herself to be one of the best of the girls she had recently employed. But the situation with James could not be allowed to develop into anything more. Wherever did he get these liberal ideas of equality? Clearly he was spending time in undesirable company.

Her opportunity was about to present itself.

Clara and Ethel were becoming unhappy with the favouritism, shown to Nellie. Too often she was needed by the family to do something special. Whenever there was time off, the girl disappeared somewhere and didn't spend time gossiping with them as she had done before.

'I don't know what she's up to, but I don't like it. Thought she was nice when she came. One of us.'

'Reckon she's sucking up to the young master. She's always going up towards his rooms. And she gets the best jobs. The easy ones like dusting the china. Why should she do it.'

'Cos you're a clumsy clutt and break things as soon as look at them.'

'No, I'm not. Well, maybe I am a bit. They break too easily. They need to make stuff stronger so it doesn't break if you drop it.'

'That reminds me, what did you do with that vase you broke?' Clara giggled.

'I moved everything else along the shelf so they wouldn't see a gap and chucked the bits in next door's rubbish. Mrs W. will never know where it went.'

'And it's usually Nellie's job to dust so they won't know it was you.' The two girls smiled conspiratorially. 'And I suppose you wouldn't know anything about the two silver teaspoons that went missing?'

'No,' replied a wide-eyed Clara. 'Think they might have found their way to the pawn shop on my last day off. It was Nellie's job to put them away.'

'Let's hope the next girl is a bit more honest, eh?'

'I've got a friend needs a job,' Clara said. 'I'll have to put in a word for her. She's all right, that one.'

'Shurrup, she's coming.'

Ethel put down her cup and smiled sweetly as Nellie came into the kitchen. 'Hello, Nellie. Where've you been for so long?'

'I've been reading.'

'Ooh, what a waste of time. We've had a lovely cuppa and a good old natter. Well, I suppose we'd better lay the dinner table. Who's in tonight?'

'How should I know?' Nellie replied.

'Thought you knew everything that goes on at the other end. Mr James is back from his trip, I gather.'

'That's right. I had to take his bag

up. Right then. What have we got to do?'

'There's some washing-up still waiting. You can get on with that before Cook sees it and complains to the Dragon Lady.' They all laughed at the words. It had really caught on. 'Hope there's something good for supper. I'm starving.'

'You can't be, Clara. You ate twice as much as the rest of us at dinner time.'

'Well, I'm a big girl with hollow legs. Takes a lot to fill me up.'

It was a couple of days later before Mrs Wilkinson noticed the missing vase. She interviewed the three maids individually and all three claimed to have no knowledge of it.

'It's usually Nellie's job to dust the china,' Ethel pointed out.

'She says she hasn't seen it for a few days.'

'Well you can't always tell when people are telling the truth. Not even you, Mrs Wilkinson. Have you noticed if anything else has gone missing?'

'Why? Do you know something?'

'No, Miss. Course not.'

The seeds were set. Mrs Wilkinson set out to make a complete inventory of the entire kitchen and dining room. She discovered the two silver teaspoons were missing and several other small items. Some of them quite valuable. She was forced to confront the mistress with her findings.

'I'm sorry, Ma'am, but it's come to my attention that several items are missing from the house. I've questioned the maids, but they all say they know nothing.'

'But you have your suspicions?'

'Nothing for sure. I don't like to make any false accusations so I won't say anything at this time. But I'd like you to check your own things in your room. There may be some pieces of jewellery missing.'

'But I always keep that in the safe.'

'With respect, Ma'am, you do sometimes leave things out.'

'Yes, but nothing of great value.

Maybe small pieces of costume jewellery.'

'Still tempting to a girl who has little to her name.'

'Very well. Please keep your eyes open and report anything suspicious to me.'

After the housekeeper left her, Mrs Cobridge began thinking. She needed James to make this trip she had discussed. This was the perfect excuse to get rid of Nellie.

Hadn't she already been dismissed from the factory through dishonesty? Once found guilty, it was easy to pin the blame on the same girl.

Mr Cobridge was more than happy for James to go on another trip. He needed some investigations into the suppliers of colours and Birmingham was a good place for looking at some of the new metallic finishes and the enamels he hoped to introduce. Unusual though for his wife to make the suggestion, but he was happy to comply.

'Very well, Father,' he agreed at dinner that night. 'But there's something I want to talk through with you. There's a new young designer I've discovered.'

'Please, James, not at the table. Can't you keep business to office hours? I want some entertaining conversation, not just china and pottery and designers and colours.'

'Sorry, my dear,' Mr Cobridge agreed. 'We weren't thinking. Oh dear, I really must do something about my digestion. I keep getting terrible cramps in my stomach.' He patted his chest in a very un-stomach like area.

★   ★   ★

James left early the next day and Mrs Cobridge sent for Nellie. She outlined her concern over the missing objects and dismissed the girl.

'I have no alternative, I'm afraid and as you already have the reputation as a thief, suspicion is naturally on you: You will have your wages to the end of the month and we shall say no more about it. I do not intend to involve the police. You may pack your things and go now. Mrs Wilkinson will give you your wages.'

'But Ma'am, I didn't take anything. I never would. I never stole anything in my life. I was sacked from the factory but it wasn't for theft. My dad would kill me if he thought I'd ever steal anything. Please, Ma'am, have pity on me. I'll never get another job.'

'That's enough. I asked to see you myself so I could explain, rather than leave it to Mrs Wilkinson. I am now rather wishing I had left it to her. I do not like unpleasantness. Now, please leave.'

Tearfully, Nellie left the room. What was it about her that always made her the one to be given the sack? She was as honest as could be and a hard worker, yet she was the one to leave.

It must have been Clara who broke the vase and threw the pieces away. It was too big for her to have stolen it. But the teaspoons the mistress had mentioned and the brooch were a different matter. Clara must have taken them and had probably pawned them.

It was so unfair. They must have been jealous because Mr James had spent time with her. She was almost certain Clara was to blame, she hesitated but decided she could say nothing.

One accusation after another would make her look even worse. There was nothing for it but to go back home. She had to face her parents and begin the thankless task of finding another job. With no references and an accusation of theft hanging over her head, there was no chance, especially these hard times. She dreaded what her father might say when she arrived home. At least Lizzie would be pleased to see her.

'Hello, love,' her mother said as she came inside. 'We weren't expecting you this evening, were we? Got another day off?'

Nellie burst into tears.

'Oh Mum, it was awful. Mrs Cobridge thinks I stole some of her things. I never did though, honest.'

'Course you didn't love. Come here.' She pulled her daughter into a warm hug. Nellie was shocked. Not only was the gesture unusual, she realised how thin her mother had become. 'I know you'd never steal a thing. Was it one of the other maids?'

'I think it was Clara. But she hasn't got a dad and her mum relies on her wage to keep her. I couldn't get her the sack, could I?'

'Maybe not, but if she got away with it once, she'll think she always can.'

'But what am I going to do? I'll never get another job.'

'Maybe this Mr James of yours will come up with something. What did he have to say about it?'

'He's gone away on a business trip.'

'So he doesn't know?'

'No, but I don't expect he'll be able to do anything. Mrs Cobridge didn't like him spending time with me. She thought it wasn't right. She's too polite to say so right out, but I could tell.' She paused and frowned at her mum. 'Are you OK? You're not looking too well and you're getting very thin again.'

'Course I'm all right. It'll be nice to have you home for a bit though. You can help me out. I must admit, I find wash days are a bit hard. But you're here now to help me. And don't worry. Something will turn up. Maybe you can do some more of your paintings. Someone might like to buy them. Now, we'll have a cuppa and then the little ones will be home from school.'

'And then Dad and Joe will be home from work. What shift are they on?

'Mornings, so they'll be home about five.'

'Let's have this tea then. I need something to give me strength. I dread to think what Dad's going to say when he hears.'

They sat companionably round the table. Nellie tried to make her mother laugh with some of the things the others had said but she felt like crying rather than laughing.

Though it had been hard work most of the time, she had enjoyed being in such lovely surroundings and having the others to share jokes. And she had to admit, Mr James had also been a very pleasant part of it all. But, it was no use dreaming. He would find some beautiful woman before long and settle down. Nellie and her pathetic little paintings would soon fade into the past.

As predicted, when Enoch came home he was furious.

'How can I believe you were innocent? It's the second time you've been sacked. No smoke without fire, I'd say.'

Nellie looked shocked and tears filled her eyes. If her own father didn't believe her, what chance did she have?

The next days were unhappy and frustrating. There seemed to be little or no work about. Nobody was taking on workers in the pot banks and nobody wanted cleaners.

The only good thing was that Nellie was able to help her mother. It was getting towards autumn and the weather was turning. Mornings were cold and the outside toilet was damp and cold and made her mother come back inside coughing badly. She dreaded the winter and having to face another long period of illness for her mother. Even her father was complaining of the cold.

'Turned reet back-endish,' he proclaimed several times a day. His injured arm was giving him more and more pain and one day he came home saying he'd been rumbled. The boss sent Joe on another job and that left him exposed.

Once they saw he couldn't work properly, they had moved him from the pit itself to a job *up top* as he called it. It was a poorly paid fetch and carry sort of job which he considered to be women's work.

'They've got me fetching cups of tea for the bosses and carting bits of paper around the place. I don't think I can stick it for long.'

'At least they gave you something instead of sacking you right off,' Nellie tried to comfort him.

'I should darned well think so. It's their fault I'm in this state in the first place. I don't know how we'll manage. You out of work as well.' He sat with his head in his hands and nobody could say or do anything to help.

'Let's have supper while we've still got something to eat,' Nan said. She was looking older and many more lines were showing on her face. 'I don't know what we've done to deserve this lot.'

'P'raps Mrs Parks will take me on as an errand boy,' Ben suggested.

'Bless you, love, but you're not even nine yet. You'll have to grow a bit before you can even get on a bike.'

★ ★ ★

Nellie might have felt a little cheered if she had been a fly on the wall at

Cobridge House. James had returned from his business trip and discovered Nellie had gone.

'How could you do it, Mother?' he demanded. 'Nellie's honest as the day is long. She'd never steal anything, and as for her breaking china. I'll never believe she'd be careless. And if she had broken something accidentally, she'd have told us about it.' He was almost shouting by the time his speech came to an end.

'James, please do not raise your voice to me. Nellie left our employment because she lied. I could not believe what she said and the other two maids both said they were innocent. We have a new girl now. A cousin or something of Ethel's. She seems quite satisfactory so far.'

'Oh, very convenient. Give one girl the sack and there just happens to be a cousin looking for work. And you believed them, but not Nellie. You don't know her like I do.'

'That's part of the problem, James. You were becoming far too familiar

154

with the girl. Quite unsuitable behaviour.'

He stared at the woman in front of him. His mother was a snob. Telling her so would do him no good at all.

'I'm going out. I shall try to find Nellie. I don't want to lose her. She had talent and I like her.'

'James, I absolutely forbid it. You can't be seen with that little . . . '

'I know, what would your precious friends say? Well, I'm sorry, Mother but I am a man now and I shall see whomever I choose. I won't be home for dinner.'

'James. Please . . . ' But he had left the room. 'Oh dear,' she sighed. 'I haven't even told him about his father.'

James Finds Nellie

James walked down the hill from his home and towards the factory. He knew Nellie was about half-an-hour away from his home, but had no idea which direction to take.

She must also live reasonably close to the factory. He wandered along countless narrow streets, where the houses were built back to back. It was quite a maze and he didn't want to knock on people's doors in an attempt to find the girl.

Some of the houses belonged to his own family, built as homes for the workers and rented out to them at reasonable rents. But Nellie's father was a miner so the chances were that she lived in one of the mine's landlords' houses.

He called in at one of the local pubs in the area, hoping to hear word of the Vale family. But his search was fruitless. He went home again and feeling peckish, visited the kitchen to see if someone would make him a sandwich.

'Mr James!' the shocked Mrs Wilkinson exclaimed. 'I'll come and see you in the drawing room.' She and the three maids were sitting round the fire drinking cocoa. It was a cosy scene and he almost wished he could be a part of it.

'I know Cook's off-duty, but I wondered of someone could make me a sandwich, please? I missed dinner this evening.'

'I'll put something on a tray and bring it to the dining room, Sir,' Mrs Wilkinson insisted.

'Thank you. Very kind. Are my parents in?'

'Yes, Sir. The Master's retired early. I think he was unwell. Your mother is in the drawing room.'

'Fine. The dining room will be

excellent. I won't disturb her. Do you think I could have some of that cocoa with my food? It smells delicious.'

'Cocoa, Sir? Wouldn't you rather have a glass of wine?'

'Cocoa, please. I haven't had it since I was a child.'

He left the room and the girls all burst out laughing.

'Fancy him wanting cocoa. I'd give anything to have a nice glass of wine. Or a port and lemon. Anything's better than cocoa,' Ethel chuckled.

'You can stop that laughing and get on with making a fresh jug. I'll see what's in the pantry for his Lordship.'

Mrs Wilkinson carried the laden tray to the dining room, anxious to speak to the young master, as he was always known. If there was something wrong, she wanted to know about it.

'Thank you. That's splendid. A feast.' He eyed the cold chicken and slice of beef and jar of pickles with delight. 'I was only expecting a sandwich, but this is marvellous. And a whole jug of cocoa. You're a marvel.'

'Ring if you need anything else, Sir. Excuse me asking, but I hope there's nothing wrong?'

'No, why should there be?'

'Well nothing, Sir. But the mistress seemed a bit out of sorts and your father did retire early after a very poor dinner for him.'

'What seems to be the trouble?'

'He was complaining of indigestion, so Ethel said after serving.'

'Eaten something that disagreed with him, no doubt.' He picked up the chicken leg and bit into it. Mrs Wilkinson stared at him in horror. That was no way for a gentleman to behave.

'Very good, Sir. I'll leave you to enjoy your meal.'

'Oh, Mrs Wilkinson, do you know where Nellie lives?'

'I'm afraid not, Sir. We didn't keep her address and as she was dismissed without references, I can't help you. Was there something in particular?'

'Not really. I just thought I'd send the paints round to her. Shame to waste them.'

'I see. Sorry I can't help.'

She went back to the kitchen. So that was it. He wanted to find that girl. The mistress certainly didn't like it.

In fact, hadn't she told the house-keeper not to discuss Nellie with Mr James? Not even if he asked anything.

Luckily, she hadn't needed to tell any fibs. She didn't know where Nellie lived, though she had a pretty good idea:

Well, well, there was more to this than met the eye. But she would say nothing to the others. They were ready enough to tattle about anything and everything without her help to add to it. All the same, it was very interesting. Maybe there had been something going on. She would never have thought of it of either of them, but nature being what it was . . .

★　★　★

The next morning, James decided to take a walk round the factory, unannounced. He liked to do this occasionally, just to see what was going on.

When he and his father made their regular tours, he suspected that things were organised to look their best. His main purpose was to visit the decorating shop to see if he could find out anything about Nellie.

One of his intentions was to ask about the Cobridge houses. He was also interested to know what sort of accommodation was provided and to throw in a casual enquiry about who lived in them. He listened to the various managers in the different departments and as soon as he could, made his way to the decorating shop. He really wanted to speak to the girls, but was immediately waylaid by Albert, the manager.

'Was there something special you wanted to know, Sir?' he asked, shooing Florence out of his office as soon as the door opened. 'Just speaking to the girl in charge of the bench,' he said as she left. She turned and flashed a smile.

'Nothing wrong?'

'No, Sir. One of our best girls is Florence.'

'Just wanted to check on the production line.'

'Certainly, Sir. Got all the orders listed here.'

James glanced over them.

'Fine. Thank you. Taken on any new girls recently?'

'No, just the same bunch. They're not a bad bunch if you keep a firm hand on them. Bit chatty at times but that's women for you. We haven't had any problems lately.'

'Good. Fine. Ever onwards.' Something was stopping him from asking after Nellie. Perhaps the office might have kept her address. He would ask down there. He didn't want anyone to be alerted by his questions.

He noticed Vera as he was leaving. She smiled up at him and he remembered she had been a friend of Nellie's and if he remembered correctly, she was the main organiser of the aborted strike at the time of Nellie's dismissal. He would speak to her after work. She must be able to help him.

When the siren went off at the end of the day, James walked to the gate, hoping to catch Vera alone. She was with a group of the women from the decorating shop. He took the plunge.

'Vera, isn't it?'

'Yes, that's right, Sir,' she replied looking somewhat alarmed.

'It's all right. I just wondered if you remembered Nellie, who used to work here?'

'Of course. Talented girl, that one. Good worker.'

'She got sent packing as a trouble maker,' chimed in Florence. 'Always causing trouble she was.'

'Shut up, Florrie. You've got no room to talk.' Several of the girls joined the group, hoping to catch a bit of gossip.

'Well, she nearly brought us all out on strike,' Florrie continued.

'And whose fault was that? I should keep your mouth shut if I were you,' Vera insisted.

'Yer, if it wasn't for you being Mr Albert's little pet, you'd be gone long ago.'

Florrie glared at the speaker and went off mumbling something about all of them being jealous. James listened to them and felt glad he wasn't a department manager. How anyone could work with a crowd like that, he'd never know. He'd had too sheltered a life, obviously. They drifted away and Vera turned and came back to speak to him.

'Excuse me asking, Sir, but I'd heard that Nellie was working up at your house. Isn't that right?'

'She was, but there was some sort of incident when I was away. I needed to contact her again.'

'I see, Sir. Well, I'm sorry I can't help you.'

'Thanks anyway. Let me know if you hear anything.'

Vera turned and walked away. She was worried. Nellie's family had enough troubles of their own without Mr. James trying to find her. He'd probably got the police out looking for her. Some sort of incident? Whatever did that mean?

She did, of course, know where the Vale family lived. She needed to call round and warn them. She'd heard the father had been moved up the pithead to work and she knew well enough what that meant as far as wages went. Drat that Florrie. She was more trouble than she was worth, but try telling that to the foolish Mr Albert. Life in the decorating shop hadn't been nearly as good since Florrie turned up.

★ ★ ★

Once she'd had supper with her husband, Vera put her coat on and went round to the Vales' house. Nellie answered the knock.

'Hello, Vera. Nice to see you, but what are you doing here? My dad's just home and he's got a right mood on him. I'd better not ask you in.'

'I've come round with a warning. Mr James, you know the young Mr Cobridge, is looking for you. He came round after work today and asked where you lived. We all cracked on we didn't know, but I thought you should know. He said as there was an incident at his place. I hope it's nothing, but I wondered if the police are involved.'

'Oh no. Not the police. I was accused of stealing, but I never did it. I know it was one of the others but as everyone else denied it I took the blame. I was last in to the house so you know how it is. Nobody can prove anything.'

'You don't have much luck, do you, girl?'

'I can't tell you how bad it is. My dad's been laid off from the pit and has to work up top for a pittance. Our Joe's still down at the bottom but he hates it. Mum's starting to be bad again and I can't get anything in the way of work. Florence did me no good when she got me the sack and nothing's gone right since.'

'Florrie was busy putting in her two penn'orth when Mr James was asking after you.'

'That's all I need. I'll just have to hide when anyone comes to the door. But thanks ever so for coming round. I'll just make something up when my dad asks who was here. It's lovely to see you. I loved working with you. Happiest time of my life, I reckon.'

'Mebbe things will work out. Best o' luck, any road up. Bye.'

'Bye, Vera. And thanks again.'

Nellie watched as she went down the road. She wished she knew why Mr James wanted her. He might just be bringing her paintings back or maybe he had been sent by his mother to get their stuff back. She sighed and went back inside, wondering what she was going to say to the family.

'Just someone I used to work with. Asking how we are,' she said lightly.

'Well, I hope you didn't tell them anything. Nobody's business but our own.'

'Course not, Dad. Why should anyone be interested in our business?'

★ ★ ★

A few days went by and there was nothing more happened. Nellie began to relax again and stopped rushing out of the back whenever a knock came to the door.

It was just like the previous time when she was out of work. She helped her mother in the house. Cooked the evening meals, trying to eke out the food as far as she could. Her mother didn't get any worse but she was still looking thin and pale.

Nellie felt guilty about all the good hearty meals she eaten at the Cobridges' house. She had put on some weight but that was rapidly disappearing again.

James cornered Vera again after work one day.

'If you've found out anything about where Nellie lives, or somewhere I could meet her, please tell me. I don't wish her any harm. Honestly, I just want to help her. I think she has got real talent and I want to help her to develop it.'

'Fond of her, are you?' Vera asked, suspicion in her voice.

'Well, yes, I suppose I am,' he said in surprise. 'Yes, I am fond of her. She's a bright girl. More intelligent than many I've come across. Much too bright to be a maid. Please help me, Vera.'

'She might never speak to me again but she lives at number fourteen Cross Street. If you cause her any trouble, I'll . . . I'll . . . '

'Don't worry, I won't. Thank you, Vera. Thank you very much. I'll go round right away.'

He left the woman standing staring

after him, her mouth wide open. She then began to worry. Had she done the right thing? It was too late now. She hadn't quite expected he'd go running straight round there. She hoped Nellie's dad wasn't home yet.

James arrived outside the little terraced house and knocked at the door. Lizzie was sent to answer, while Nellie stood behind the curtains watching to see who it was.

When she saw James standing outside, she hissed at her little sister.

'Tell him I'm out. You don't know when I'll be back.'

'Hello. I'd like to speak to Nellie, please.'

'She says she's out and I'm to tell you I don't know when she'll be back.'

James grinned.

'Well, please tell her I'll wait at the end of the street. I must see her soon.'

Lizzie shut the door and he stood back. He'd seen the curtain twitch and knew she was listening. He walked away and turned and came back. He knocked again. Another twitch of the curtain. This time Nellie's mother answered.

'Hello. Mrs Vale? I'm James Cobridge. You daughter used to work for us.'

'My daughter wouldn't ever steal anything. I've brought her up to be a decent girl. Goes to chapel every Sunday, well, when she's at home that is.'

'I know she's honest. It was my mother who dismissed her. It was when I was away or I'd have spoken up for her. Please ask her to see me. I really want to help her and we both know she is talented. I don't want to see it go to waste. Besides, I'm very fond of her. Please, Mrs Vale.'

'She still won't see you, I'm afraid. But I'll pass on your message.'

'Very well. Thank you. But . . . oh, never mind.' He looked crestfallen as he turned away. Nan watched him and felt sorry for her rejection.

'Our Nellie? You can come out now. I think he's good 'un, you know, love. I don't think he means you any harm.'

171

'I'll never forgive Vera and the others. They must have let on they knew our address. Now he knows where we live, he'll probably never come again. Horrible little street. Miserable little house. Bit of a long way from what he's used to.'

'Our Nellie, this isn't like you. Sounds as though you're ashamed of us. We do our best. Always have done. Seems to me you've got ideas beyond yourself.'

'Oh, I'm sorry, Mum. I'm just that worried. And I'd got used to decent, regular meals. I'm not complaining . . . not really but I'd thought things were coming right for us. Now it seems we've gone from bad to worse.'

Nan began another coughing fit and went back into the kitchen to sit down near the fire. 'I'm sorry, Mum. I shouldn't have let you stand out in the cold. Shall I make you a hot drink?'

'It's all right, love. I think I might go to bed. Your dad won't be back for ages and I do feel worn out.'

'Call me if you want anything. Night, Mum.'

Nellie watched her mother climb the stairs as wearily as if she had been down the mines all day. It was very worrying as it wasn't even winter yet and she was always worse in the very cold weather. If only she could get a decent job, she could buy food and medicine to help her mother.

* * *

The next evening, James came again. He knocked on the door and this time, Nan made her daughter answer it. She cast her eyes down and refused to look him in the eye.

'Nellie. Thank you for seeing me. Don't be afraid. I know what my mother did. I know you're honest and if she was equally honest, she knows she made a mistake.'

'Then why did she have to go and sack me?'

'I suspect she was afraid that I was

getting too involved with you.'

'How do you mean involved?'

'She could see that I was beginning to take too much interest in you. And yes, that I was beginning to care for you a little too much.'

'You? Care for me? Don't be daft. You live in a different world to mine. You've got the pick of anyone in society. Good looking young man like you. Wealthy family. Posh house. Look at me. Look where I come from. I'm not even good enough to be a servant in your . . . your posh house.' She paused for breath, her face quite pink with anger.

'Nellie, you are a wonderful girl. My mother was right to be concerned. No, don't look like that. For now though, I just want you to come and work at the factory. You'll work for me, personally. I want you as part of the group of designers. I'll set aside space near my office for you to work and you'll have a decent wage. I'll have to sort that out with the accounts department.'

'Really? But what's in it for you?'

'I get a talented paintress who is going to help drive us forward into a bright future. Now, are you going to introduce me to your family?'

'I will soon, Sir, but my mum's been took . . . taken badly. She's really poorly and not up to having visitors.'

'Two things. First drop the Sir. I'm James. And secondly, I want to know what is wrong with your mother. I may be able to help.'

'I don't know how you can help. But all right then. You can come round tomorrow evening. Our tea's usually over and done with by half-past six. Then you'll have time to get back for your own dinner. Just don't expect too much.'

'Thank you, Nellie.'

'I don't think I'll ever be able to call you James. Mrs Wilkinson would skin me alive.'

'Fortunately, this has nothing to do with the Dragon Lady.'

Slowly, Nellie began to grin and then she laughed.

'Oh, Sir, I can't help thinking what she might say if she knew what you called her.'

'Sir?'

'Mr James then. That's as far as I can manage.'

'Very well. I'll call again at six-thirty tomorrow.'

Nellie spent the next day cleaning and scrubbing the floors. The house looked as clean as it could but she was always conscious of the differences between Mr James and her own situation.

He really could have no idea of what her home life was like. She persuaded her mother to spend the day in bed, hoping the rest would do her good. She came down at four o'clock, dressed in her Sunday best.

'Thought I should try to make an effort. My, everywhere looks lovely and clean. You have been working hard. I'd better start on tea.'

'I've done it already. Made a suet pudding. It's on the stove boiling nicely.

Makes the meat go much further with some pastry round it and I thought it might put my dad in a good mood. I don't want him sounding off in front of Mr James.'

'I don't know why he has to come, any road. He's only offering you a job, isn't he?'

'Course he is. What else would he want with the likes of me? Although, he said his mother was concerned that he was taking too much interest in me. What do you think that meant?'

'Oh, Nellie, you're such a kid really, aren't you?'

'I'm nineteen.'

'You just don't know what men can be like, do you? She's worried he might try to have his way with you.'

'Don't be daft. I do know some things, you know. I'm just a skinny little girl. Men won't ever be interested in me. Not like that.'

'Just be careful, love. Now, how about a cuppa while we wait for the kids to come home.'

As she spoke, Lizzie and Ben came clattering in through the back scullery door.

'Take your mucky shoes off and don't make a mess. I've spent all day cleaning.'

'Is there anything to eat?' Ben demanded.

'You can wait for your tea.'

'But I'm starving,' he protested.

'Well, carry on starving. You can always suck your thumb like our Lizzie.'

'It's not fair. Other kids get fed when they get home.'

'Life's not fair, Ben. Now, go and play out or go up to your room. Mum and I are having a cup of tea.'

'Can we have one?' asked Lizzie.

'Oh, go on then. Just a small one. You don't even like it much. Get your mugs.'

Tea was on the table when Joe and Enoch came home. They washed the mine grime off themselves and sat down.

'This looks good. Always did manage

a good meal, did your mum,' Enoch said.

'Our Nellie made it, all by herself.'

'Good girl. You'll be able to take a load off your mum while she's poorly.'

'Dad, you haven't forgotten that Mr James is coming round this evening? He's offered me a job and wanted to meet you before I start.'

'Can't think what for. Business is business. Nothing to do with us. Just make sure he gives you a decent wage.'

'I don't know why he wants to meet you all, but he says he does, so what can I do? I really want this job. It's everything I could have dreamed of. He says he'll pay a decent wage as well. More than I was getting before.'

'Sounds all right, but you are a woman. Painting china isn't real work, is it?' Joe remarked.

Nellie scowled at him.

'You should try painting a great long line of cups every day. Apart from having the talent, a steady hand and good eyesight, bits of you ache with staying in one position. And the pay is hardly great. Better than being a maid in a posh house and working your fingers to the bone all day, though.'

'Yer, but you got your meals on top. And a uniform.'

'Finish your tea, our Joe, and then smarten yourself up a bit. Our Nellie's worked hard today ready for the boss to come round. We don't want him thinking we're nobodies.'

'Which we are,' Nellie said anxiously. 'Now, I'll clear the table. Lizzie, Ben, you can help dry the pots.'

When the chores were finished, Nellie went up to her room and combed her hair. She smoothed down her dress and kept her fingers crossed. Why did Mr James have to put them through this?

His knock sounded at the door. Almost shaking, she went to let him in.

A Return To The Factory

Nellie brought him through to the cosy kitchen and offered him a seat next to the fire.

'James Cobridge,' he said holding out his hand first to Nan and then Enoch. 'Pleased to meet you.'

Her parents muttered something indistinguishable and held out nervous hands.

'This is Joe, Ben and little Lizzie, my brothers and sister.' Lizzie tugged at Nellie's skirt.

'I'm not little Lizzie, any more. I'm six and three-quarters and I go to school.'

'I can see you're not little any more, Lizzie. And what do you like doing best at school?'

'Sums. And writing but I'm not very good at it.'

Nellie listened in amazement. Her little sister hardly ever said much and never to strangers. Mr James certainly had a way with him.

'It's good of you to allow me to call,' he said confidently. 'Nellie tells me you haven't been well, Mrs Vale?'

'No, Sir. I gets it every winter, not that it's proper winter yet. I've started with my cough early this year. It's the damp.'

He glanced round the room and noticed that despite the obvious cleaning regime, and the warm fire, there were patches on the walls that must result from a damp climate.

'And Mr Vale, I gather you sustained an injury in a mining accident?'

'Yes, Sir. Damaged my arm and now I can't work down the pit. They've given me something up at the pit head but that doesn't pay me anything like working down the bottom.'

'Well, I'd like to do something to help. As you know, I'm hoping Nellie will come and work at the factory again, for a decent wage. But that will only help part of the way. I have an uncle who is a very well respected doctor in Burslem. I'm asking him to give you an appointment . . . in fact, better still, I shall ask him to call round. I expect you find bus journeys tedious. I'm certain he'll be able to help. And he can look at your arm too, Mr Vale. Might as well while he's here.'

'I'm sorry, Sir. It's good of you to take an interest, but we simply can't afford any doctors to call.'

'There will be no charge. I'll ask him to do it as a favour. Any medicines he recommends will also be without charge, of course.'

Nellie listened and looked at her parents. It was very tempting to think her mother might be relieved of her many afflictions but they simply could not accept charity.

'Thank you, Sir,' she said angrily. 'But we don't need charity from you or anyone else.'

'Don't think of it as charity at all.

Your parents need help. I can provide it. Besides, it's as much for you as them. I want you free to work for me and not having to care for your family. Nor do I want you worrying about them while you're at work. There will be times when your hours may be long and you may need to travel a little. Be away overnight, occasionally.'

'Exactly what are you suggesting?' Enoch demanded.

'Nothing, Sir. I'm not suggesting anything untoward. I assure you, my motives are completely honourable.'

'I don't fall for none of your fancy talk. My Nellie's a good girl. She's a bit, well, doesn't know much about the ways of the world.'

'I'm very fond of your daughter. I can assure you that I would never do anything to hurt her. Not in any way.'

'I think you should go now, Sir,' Nellie told him trying to hide her blushes. She wasn't used to compliments and didn't know how to handle it. All the same, she didn't like the idea of them being a charity case, whatever he said.

'I've told you, it's in my own interests to make sure that your family are well cared for. I hope I might even be a part of this family one day.'

Nellie's mouth dropped open even further.

'I don't know what you're suggesting. I'm very pleased you've offered me a good job, I'm pleased to accept but as for the rest, whatever it is, I'm just a working girl. I don't fit into your family and never could. Your mother would have a fit if she knew you were even thinking of me as anything more than a maid or a paintress. Thank you for calling. I'll show you out.'

'There's plenty of time, Nellie. I shall see you on Monday. Can you remember where my office is? Eight o'clock, please.'

'Very well, Sir. Thank you.' She led him through the dingy parlour, never used and sparsely furnished. He caught her hand.

'I thought we were dropping the *Sir*? At least in private.'

'If I'm to work at the factory, it simply wouldn't do. The other girls would think it was favouritism. They'd treat me really badly. Believe me, I know.'

He smiled a dazzling smile at her and touched her under the chin. She felt as if her heart was about to jump out of her chest.

'You won't be working with the rest of the girls. But if you insist. *Mr James* will have to do and once we have spent time together, you will soon get used to calling me James. By the way, this house you live in. It isn't one of our places, is it?'

'No, Sir. It's one of the mine owners' places. Why do you ask?'

'We do rent out some houses. If this was one of ours, I would need to get some repairs done for you. You have a few problems with damp. Not really healthy for your mother. Ah well. Few things are perfect in this life. I'll say goodbye now. I look forward to seeing you on Monday.'

'Goodbye. And thanks again.'

She watched him walk away. He was a splendid figure of a man and if she allowed herself to think about it, she could dream about him very easily. It was all futile. She went back inside and shut the door. She went slowly back to the kitchen and took a deep breath, ready to face her family.

'You need to think carefully, our Nellie,' her father announced.

'Oh, I am. I'm not sure why Mr James is making all these offers of help. I'm no catch for him so I can only believe the worst might happen.'

'I'm not sure what you think is the worst. You want to snap him up, that's what I'm saying. Whatever he's offering, you take it. You'll never get a chance like this again. Take whatever you can get and whatever it costs, it has to be worth it.'

'Dad? What ever are you suggesting?'

'You're not that stupid, girl. You

might hold out for a legal marriage but if he's offering something, take it. You owe it to all of us.'

'I can't believe you're saying this. Mum, tell him. I can't just . . . I can't do just anything he asks.'

'I don't know, love. You have to do what you think is right. But I think I understand what your Dad's saying. If we can get a doctor to see us and it makes life better, we won't have to be poor for ever. It's a great opportunity for you.'

'I'll have to think. I'm going upstairs. It almost feels like my own father is trying to sell me to the highest bidder.'

'Nellie!' Nan called after her.

She lay on her bed and Lizzie came to lie beside her. The child snuggled close and put her arm over her big sister.

'Are you cross with me?' she whispered.

'No, darling. Why should I be?'

'Cos I said I wasn't a little girl to your sir.'

'Oh, Lizzie, course not. I'm just feeling a bit upset. But mostly, I'm tired. I had a really busy day. Now, why don't you get yourself ready for bed now. We can settle down together and I can tell you a story.'

'Ooh, yes please. Will it have a beautiful princess and a handsome prince?'

'Yes indeed. The most beautiful one you've ever heard of.'

★   ★   ★

It was a restless night and Nellie went downstairs early the next morning, to leave Lizzie sleeping for a while longer. There was no question in her mind that she was going to accept James's offer of work.

She couldn't have wished for a better chance. She would be paid to spend her day painting china again and she would be able to do some new designs. Her mind whirled over the possibilities that would be open to her. She would be

189

bringing in a wage that would help the family. What was there to doubt? If he wanted to send a doctor to them, why should she worry? For her mother's sake, she really shouldn't object and she had to forget her stupid pride. It wasn't charity after all.

She would work very hard and it would all be payment for what she was going to do. She put some coal on the fire and set the kettle to boil on the hob. Everyone would be coming down soon for their breakfast and another day was beginning.

★　★　★

The rest of the week went slowly for Nellie. She couldn't wait till Monday. Her parents were delighted that she was starting a job she liked and her father kept asking how much she thought she'd be earning.

'I really don't know yet, Dad. Mr James had to see the accounts department. Did I say as I don't have to start work till eight o'clock. It used to be seven o'clock. It's almost as if I'm staff. They never start till eight.'

'Yes, love. You've told us,' her mother laughed. Even she was looking better at the prospect of a bit more money coming into the house.

'Do you reckon you can get me a job with some prospects?' Joe asked. 'I hate it down the pit.'

'I'm not sure you'd like it any better at the pot bank. Most of the chaps are working in heat and it's dusty and dirty, just like the pits.'

'At least it's white dust instead of black,' he muttered. 'And it's light. This time of year, I never see daylight. It's dark when I go down and dark down there and then, oh yes, it's dark when I come home.'

'Shame you skipped off school so much then, isn't it? If you'd done a bit more learning, you might have got a better job.'

'What's the point? I have to keep this family. When our Nellie's earning her great big wages, maybe I can think of doing something else.'

When Monday finally arrived, Nellie was ready to leave much earlier than she needed. She packed her bag with her old mug, an apron she'd made out of an old skirt and a slice of bread and dripping for her lunch.

She felt a bit embarrassed at the bread and dripping. If James saw what she ate, he might made some comment. But it was all there was and she could always eat it when he was working in his office.

She arrived at the lodge.

'Morning, George,' she said with a big smile.

'Hello, love. Well, what a surprise. Come to see the girls, have you?'

'No, I'm back permanent, like. I'm to be working for Mr James so I don't start with the rest. Don't you want to look in my bag?'

'Well, no. I suppose not. If you're working for Mr James, I s'pose you'd best go straight up. It's a right treat to see you again. How's that mother of yours?'

'Oh, you know. Up and down. Not so good now winter's coming again. I'd better get up there. I'm not even sure exactly where to go.'

'Up the stairs and turn right. His office is on the left. Second door. Good luck then. I'll mention it to Vera, shall I? I'm sure she'll want to see you.'

'I'll catch up later. I suppose Florence hasn't left by any good luck, has she?'

'Not that one. She knows where her bread's buttered. Nasty piece of work but she's got her boss exactly where she wants him. Keep well away from that one, mark my words.'

'I will. Thanks, George. See you later.'

The offices were situated in a rather dark, oak lined corridor. It was very different from the rest of the factory. She saw the door to James's office and tapped gently.

'Come in.'

Timidly, she turned the handle and opened the door. Mr James was sitting behind an enormous desk covered in papers. 'Nellie. Lovely to see you. Come and sit down.' She perched on the edge of a large leather chair feeling very shy and quite out of place. 'How are your parents?'

'Well, thank you, Sir.'

'Don't look so frightened. Are they really well? Your mother?'

'No, Sir. She's a bit poorly today. But I got the others off to work and school and having a bit later start, meant she could stay in bed for a while and rest. Thanks for asking, Sir.'

'You know, it's going to be hard work if you're going to look so terrified and I hate this *Sir* nonsense.'

'I can't help it. I'm not used to calling you anything else. If it's all the same to you, I'd like to start my work now. Where am I to go?'

'Ah, yes. Your work place. It's not very grand but you can use the room through here.'

He opened a door at one side of the office. It was little more than a large cupboard but there was a window and a bench down one side. 'I had a secretary at one time and she used this space. We decided I didn't need her, though, and now there's just one secretary for me and my father. Do you think you'll manage in here?'

'It's lovely, but it's a bit posh for me to use for painting pottery. That's an oak bench. It's lovely, polished wood.'

'We can put a piece of board over it if you prefer. But you'll be using pencil and paper and paints to do some of the designs. We're going to need another table for you, aren't we? I'll get one of the men to bring one up. And the chair? Will it be comfortable enough for you to work?'

'It's beautiful. I've never sat on such a lovely chair.'

'Now, I've brought your water-colour paints in and lots of paper. There's a drawing board for you and I've asked for a pile of white plates and cups to be brought up. There's a selection of colours, linseed and turps and a pot of brushes. Anything else you can think of?'

'I think you've got everything. What am I supposed to paint on the china?'

'Anything you like. Let your imagination go wild. My mother loved your fairy paintings. Try something like that on the larger plates. And the all over floral patterns. She liked them, especially the pastel shades. For me, I loved some of the bold and bright things. Just do whatever takes your fancy.'

'Really? Really, just anything I like?'

James nodded, smiling at her growing enthusiasm.

'There's a kettle in the little kitchen. I'll show you. Make tea whenever you want it. There are cups and things in there. And biscuits. Help yourself. If there's anything you like better, just ask. Mrs Wiley looks after us very well.'

'I've brought my own mug in. Like we always did in the decorating shop.'

'I don't think you'll be needing that.

And we usually have sandwiches brought up at lunch time. I ordered one for you, if that's all right.'

'I don't know what to say. It's all like a dream.'

'Just show me how well you can work. Make some beautiful designs for us. I have to go to a meeting now. Make yourself at home. I'll see you later on.'

Nellie sat at her desk and pulled out the folder of her old paintings. She was surprised he had kept them and was pleased to see that some were better than she remembered. She began to work, excited at the prospects that lay ahead.

It was very quiet up there and she rather missed the banter of the other girls and a noisier environment. It was all very different from anything she had known before. Someone knocked at her door. She went to answer it. A cheery little woman stood there.

'Hello, dearie. I've brought you a cuppa. Mr James said as how you was working in here. Bit cramped, isn't it?

Oh, I'm Mrs Wiley, by the way.'

'Oh, Nellie Vale. How do you do?' She held out a paint covered hand and then pulled it back. 'Sorry, I'm a bit messy.'

'Them your pictures?' she asked. Nellie nodded. 'Very nice. You're a clever little thing, aren't you? No wonder Mr James has taken a shine to you.'

'He has? Well, yes, he's been very kind to me. Thank you for the tea.'

'Help yourself whenever you want a cup. And there's plenty of cups. I always wash up when I come in so no need to clear up after yourself. None of them do.' She nodded towards the other offices.

'Does Mr Cobridge come in every day?'

'He often comes in of an afternoon. But he's been poorly lately. Dunno what's up with him, but he hasn't been in for a week or two now. Mr James is seeing to everything. Nice talking, but I'd best get on now or her down there will be after me. She's the secretary. Right *la-di-dah* she is. Nothing to be so stuck up about. I knew her mother years ago and she was no better than she ought to be.'

Nellie smiled. She said nothing. If in her world of fantasy she ever did get together with Mr James, everyone would say the same things about her. Not that her mother had ever done anything to be ashamed, of, but she certainly did have a background of poverty.

She sipped the tea from a bone china cup, for the first time. It didn't taste quite the same as her old mug and it had cooled very quickly. The cup was one made in the factory, of course.

She studied the pattern. It wasn't one she knew and she wondered how it could all be so regular. She looked more closely. The flowers were definitely hand-painted but the borders seemed to be sort of flatter on the saucer. She glanced up as the door opened and James came in.

'What do you think of that?' he asked.

'I was wondering how they got the border so even. I think the flowers are hand-painted.'

'Quite right, It's a transfer. A sort of printed sheet that's applied to the saucer and the paper is peeled off, leaving the design. This is then filled in with the colours as you see. Surely you've seen them being made?'

'No, Sir . . . Mr James. I haven't seen anywhere other than the decorating shop. The one I worked in, with Vera and the rest.'

'Haven't any of you been round the factory?'

'Not that I know of. I used to go to the stores to collect the paints and the stock room next to our shop.'

'So you don't know about the manufacturing process at all? Transfers? Aerographing?'

'No, Sir. We never even saw it coming out of the kilns. Well, we saw the saggers when they were taken out but it was too blinkin' hot to stand too near them.'

The large fireclay containers, the saggers, were used to stand the ware in for firing were stacked in high piles in the bottle kilns and once the heat had died back a little, were unloaded. As they were coming in to work, the girls were always aware of the immense heat. It was good to walk a bit closer when it was a cold winter morning.

'I think we need to make a trip round the whole factory, so you can see the process from start to finish. Would you like that?'

'Oh, yes please.' The mysteries of how the clay turned into the beautiful china would all be answered.

'Very well. Tomorrow morning, we shall make a tour. Maybe I should think about letting some of the others see round. What do you think? Would they be interested?'

'I think so but they'd worry about loss of earnings. Don't forget, they're on piece work rates. If they don't make up the numbers, they get less in the wage packets at the end of the week.'

'I could make it a voluntary thing. Perhaps on a Saturday?'

'They'll all want to get home after the morning. The married ones have to get dinners ready and the men usually go to watch the match. Either Port Vale or Stoke City.'

'I suppose so. Now, how have you been getting on?'

'I'm sorry, but I don't seem to have done much. I was looking at some of the paintings I did and trying to improve on them. Some of the things like the fairies would be difficult to put on to anything other than plates. And they'd take so long to do, they'd be very expensive.'

'Good girl.' James was surprised by her thinking process. 'So, they would have to be our collector's plates. Haven't you seen that range?'

'No. Why would people just collect plates? They wouldn't match anything else. Cups and saucers, I mean.'

'Don't you remember the plates in the china cupboard at home? Fruit and flower paintings?'

'Oh, I see. I thought they were just samples or something. Like pictures, they are.'

'Indeed so. They are collected just as ornaments and will gain in value in time. But I'm thinking they can be made as lithographs . . . transfers and the painting finished by hand if necessary.'

'There's such a lot I don't know. What's the aerogr . . . something you mentioned?'

'Aerograph. It's when they spray a whole piece with colour so you have something of just one block colour. Spraying it means it's a much more even finish. I'll show you everything tomorrow. Now, I need to spend some time with the managers down at the clay end. A few problems looming. Oh yes, I had a word with the accounts department. You'll be getting four pounds and sixteen shillings for the time being.'

'Four pounds and sixteen shillings?' she gasped. But that's nearly as much as Joe gets down the pits. Are you sure? I don't know if I'm worth that much.'

'You'll have to work hard to prove it then, won't you? You're worth every penny of it to me.' He went off and she heard his office door close.

Nellie sat staring at her pictures. How could she be worth that sort of money? She felt nervous and wondered if she would ever be able to produce anything so special to make it worth paying her that much.

She remembered what one of the maids had said at the Cobridge house. Don't tell them exactly how much you're earning and save a bit for yourself. She was right. If her dad knew how much she was getting, he'd only spend more of his own money down at the Miners' Social Club and the family would be no better off. It was a difficult one. But she was going to need to buy herself some new clothes for a start.

Her old working dress would hardly do for someone who earned four pounds and sixteen shillings a week. She heard another knock and called, 'Come in.'

She didn't want to put down her brush at that point, even though her call sounded a bit rude. Sidney came in, the boy from the shop where they stored the finished white china.

'Wotcha, Nellie,' he said. 'They said as you was back.'

'Sidney. Nice to see you.'

'My, you've gone up the world.'

'I have, haven't I?'

'I've been told to bring some white ware for you to paint. Dunno why you has to have it up here. Why aren't you in the decorating shop with the others?'

'I'm designing some new stuff. I need to practise it to get it right before it's introduced to the others. Anyway, thanks for bringing it up.'

'Nellie,' he began. He blushed and turned his eyes away. 'Nothing.'

'Go on, Sidney. You were going to say?'

'Nothing. You wouldn't be interested. Not now you've moved up here.' She stared at him. She remembered Vera once saying Sidney was interested in her.

'Say hello to the girls for me,' she said with a warm smile. Even if he was interested in her, she had indeed moved on.

She picked up her new tile and looked along the array of paints. Mr James wanted something modern and spectacular, she'd give it to him. She flicked through her pages of paintings and found a bold orange design, with black and green swirls.

She picked up one of the delicate plates and began to put on the paint. She laughed to herself as she used a large brush to add a great sweep of colour. When she had finished one plate, she picked up another and painted a series of squares, linked together at the corners. She could never remember enjoying herself more.

The results may have looked very different to anything she had ever done before, but the plates were something quite new. By the end of the afternoon, she had a line of brightly coloured designs, some of which she was pleased with and others she didn't like at all. She was about to wipe the colour off when James came in

'Wow, these are spectacular. Very different. Nellie Vale, you're doing exactly what was needed.' He flung his arms round her and danced her round the tiny room, practically crashing into the chair and desk at the same time.

Breathlessly, she almost fell into her chair, Mr James hanging onto the edge of the desk to regain his balance. 'Very well worth your wages.'

'I'm glad you like them. I wasn't sure about these,' she said holding up the ones she had been about to clean off.

'We'll get them all fired and see how they look after that.'

'But if they may be wasted because

nobody likes them . . . '

'Don't worry about it. We all have to learn and progress.'

'But if we spoiled a plate or cup or anything, it got knocked off our wages at the end of the week. In fact, it was a couple of cracked pieces that got me the sack in the first place.'

'Oh dear, you make me realise how little I know of the workings of this place. One day, I shall review the whole thing. I am very worried about living conditions as well as the working conditions. You'll see for yourself tomorrow when we go round. Some shops are dreadful places to work. What happens to people when they are too ill to work any more? It all worries me considerably.'

'You're a good man for a . . . ' She paused.

'For a boss?' Nellie smiled and said no more.

He was a good man. She was becoming a bit too fond of someone so out of her reach.

A Shocking Announcement

Nellie's tour round the factory opened her eyes considerably. She had never known there were so many processes before the finished white china arrived on the benches. Nor had she realised the terrible dust, smells and dangerous processes that went on.

The dust in the room where pieces from the kilns were unpacked was choking. The workers there were covered from top to toe in the white powder.

When they arrived in her old decorating shop, there were many greetings called, until they saw she was accompanied by Mr James himself. She felt very awkward and could only speak to Vera and one or two of the others who had been sympathetic. Florrie was of course in Mr Albert's office and came out looking slightly guilty that Mr James had noticed her.

'Is that girl all right?' he asked the manager privately in the office.

'Florrie? She's fine. Great girl. Why do you ask?'

'She always seems to be in your office when I come to this department.'

'She helps give me the numbers each week. Very good girl. Nice with it. Very popular with others too. Useful to have a contact with the girls. You know what they're like.'

James looked sceptical. He had his own source of information in Nellie. He would ask her about Florrie's popularity. He was certain there was something going on between her and his manager and she was not passing on working numbers each week. He went back to the work room and nodded to Nellie that he was ready to move on. She said her goodbyes and they went back to the office upstairs.

'I'll get these plates collected and fired. I hope to introduce a few new lines very soon. Did you enjoy your tour?'

'Yes, it was really very interesting. I think I know a lot more now.'

'Good. That was the purpose if it. By the way, what do you know about the girl, Florrie?' Nellie looked away. What on earth could she say about her old enemy?

'Florrie? Er, well, she's not a bad paintress.'

'Is she something special to Albert?'

'Well, they see quite a bit of each other, I think. The others say he takes her for a drink after work some days.'

'I see. It's like that, is it? And how does she feel about you?'

'Me? I don't think she likes me very much. She was always a bit jealous cos I got to paint a lot of the new patterns when they came in.'

'And so she would be even more jealous if she knew your new role in the scheme of things?'

'I expect so.'

'Was she the cause of you being

fired?' he asked rather bluntly. Nellie hesitated. She didn't want to cause even more trouble than there had been. 'Well? Was she?'

'Well, yes. She told tales to Mr Albert, I'm sure. I'd rather not say any more, though.'

'Nellie Vale, you're just too good a person for a place like this. The thing is though, once we get some of your designs into production, you're going to have to go back to the decorating shop to oversee them at first. Will you manage that?'

'I'll have to, won't I? What has to be done has to be done. Vera and them will always back me. Mind you, I haven't forgiven her for letting on to you where I lived.'

'Good job she did or you wouldn't be here now.' He touched her shoulder and smiled down at her. 'Oh, by the way. I've arranged for my uncle, you know, the doctor, to call on your mother today. I hope he will be able to help her.'

'That's very good of you. But I wish you'd let me know. My mum will be all of a dither if he just turns up.'

James laughed.

'He's used to all sorts. Don't worry.' She frowned slightly and he smoothed the wrinkles away. 'You're turning into a very pretty woman, you know. May I ask how old you are now?'

'I'll be twenty in a week's time.'

'Then we must celebrate the occasion. I'd like to take you out for dinner.'

'What? To a proper restaurant?'

'If you'd like that. I would invite you home but I doubt my mother would welcome that arrangement.' Nellie giggled.

'And I don't think Ethel would like to serve me at the table, either.'

'Then a restaurant it is.'

'Thank you very much. But I should warn you, I haven't ever been to a restaurant. S'pose I don't know what to do?'

'You just follow me. Don't worry about it. I want you to enjoy it and let it be a treat for you.'

'What will I wear?' she suddenly thought out loud.

'Something fairly smart . . . ' He paused. Did Nellie have anything smart? He'd only seen her in her working clothes or maid's uniform. Perhaps he was putting her in a difficult situation. 'I expect you've got a Sunday best?' She nodded. 'Then that will be fine.' He knew her family were chapel goers so she would always dress up for that. 'I'll book somewhere for next . . . which day is it?'

'Next Tuesday.'

'That's a date.'

'Thank you, Mr James.'

'One condition.'

'I know. I have to call you James.'

He smiled and nodded as he left the room. Nellie's smile wrapped right round her face for the rest of the day.

★ ★ ★

'Why didn't you tell me a doctor was coming here today?' Nan challenged her when she got home.

'I didn't know he was coming till Mr James told me this afternoon. What did he say?'

'He's going to get me some special medicine to take whenever I cough. And I've got have better food. No more eating what's left over from the rest of you. He doesn't think it's anything too terrible so that's a relief. It isn't anything terminal.'

'Thank goodness.'

They talked about how she should cope during the winter and agreed that she must use more of Nellie's wages to feed herself properly. Nellie told her mother about the promised birthday outing.

* * *

By the day of her birthday, Nellie was a gibbering wreck of nerves. Why had she ever agreed to go out with James? Her Sunday best frock was a dreadful old thing. She thought about the dresses

James's mother wore just for dinner in their own home.

They were grander than anything she had ever seen before. She would have to tell him she was unwell. Tell him she was sick or something. If she took the day off work, she needn't see him. But in the end, her conscience wouldn't let her.

She went to work as always and escaped to her little room without being seen. On her desk was a large box, tied with a ribbon. Was it really for her? There was nothing on it to indicate that it was but for who else could it be, left on her very own desk.

With trembling fingers, she untied the ribbons and lifted the lid. There was a card lying on top of the tissue paper.

To Nellie, Wishing you a happy birthday. With fondest regards, James.

Fondest regards. She went pink. She lifted the tissue and saw a dress lying inside. It was a soft blue silky dress with a lace collar and possibly the most beautiful thing she had ever seen, for a dress that was. She lifted it carefully from the box, letting it hang against her. It looked as if it would fit perfectly. She held it against her and twirled round. It was perfect.

'Oh good, you found it. I hope you like it?'

'It's beautiful, perfect.'

'Will it fit, do you think?'

'Oh yes, it looks just right. How clever of you.'

'I asked Ethel for the size of your old uniform. I didn't want to get anything too modern, I wasn't sure any of these Charleston dresses would be quite you. Not yet anyway.'

'I'm not even sure I know what you mean?'

'Will you wear it tonight for me?'

'Of course. I didn't really know what to wear, so this is perfect.'

'I think so. I planned it all. It matches your eyes. I shall look forward to it. I will call for you at seven o'clock. I am borrowing my father's car for the occasion. I really must get a car of my own very soon. Just a small one.'

'Oh, James. This is the most exciting of my life. A new dress. Dinner in a restaurant and riding in a car. Whoever would have thought little Nellie Vale could rise to this?'

'And you even called me James without thinking.'

* * *

It was almost ten o'clock when she was delivered home. With shining eyes, she said goodnight to James. He opened her door and helped her out of the car. He gave her a kiss on the cheek and touched her shoulder.

'Thank you for the most wonderful birthday I ever had.'

'Here's to many more spent together. Good night, Nellie. See you in the morning.'

She watched him drive away and turned to go into her house. She noticed several curtains twitching as the neighbours watched the unaccustomed sight of a car leaving their street.

'What was it like, love?' her mother asked anxiously. She had been worrying all night in case Nellie couldn't manage everything.

'It was lovely, Mum. We went to a hotel. An actual hotel. There were flowers on every table. Real ones with proper water in the vases. And white serviettes the waiter put on our knees.'

'Sounds like a waste of money,' grumbled Enoch.

'So what did you have to eat?' Nan asked, her eyes shining at the thought of it all.

'There was soup to begin. It was made from celery. Quite tasty but it felt funny eating white soup. Then there was duck with vegetables. That was lovely. Best of all was the pudding. It was a chocolate sort of mousse, he said it was, with a chocolate shortcake underneath. They put a candle on it and I had to blow it out. For my birthday, you know. I had a very small glass of wine with the meal. I didn't like that much but I couldn't really say no, could I?'

'As long as you don't get the taste for it. It's all right occasionally, I suppose.' Nan was a little concerned for her daughter. 'And don't go getting expensive tastes. And I'm not sure I approve of a gentleman buying clothes for someone who isn't his wife.'

'Nothing wrong with it as I can see,' Enoch pronounced. 'Better he should buy her something useful, though.'

'Make sure you hang it up properly. Keep it nice. He might ask you to go out again one day.'

★　★　★

There was another surprise for Nellie at work the next day. The plates she had painted with the bold designs, were waiting on her desk. Bright and glossy, they looked most striking. She picked them up and examined them carefully. They were still slightly warm from the kiln. Some of the paint looked less smooth than she liked but they certainly were very different.

'What do you think?' James asked as he arrived in his office.

'I quite like them. The orange is a bit sort of lumpy in places, but I don't think they're too bad.'

'I love them. I think they are just what we need to steal a march on our competitors. I need you to do some cups and saucers now and we'll get them in the next firing. I'm going on a sales trip next week and I want to introduce them as our new line. With a bit of luck, we might do something for the Christmas market. Perhaps you should come with me? What do you say?'

'I don't think my parents would let me go away with a man. Not to stay away.'

'Don't worry. You can trust me, I should like you with me to talk to the buyers. In fact, we'll take my secretary as a chaperone. We would stay at a decent hotel, not my usual salesman's digs.'

'Can I think about it? I'll talk to my mother and see what she thinks.'

'Fine, but I need to know by tomorrow so I can book. See what you can do with the cups and saucers to match the plates now. I'll get some sent up to you.'

There was quite a discussion that evening at the Vale supper table. Two concerned parents warned their daughter about the dangers of strange places and strange hotels, though neither of them had any experience at all.

Her mother seemed more concerned than her father. She suspected he was still thinking of an easier life in future if Nellie was hitched up with her boss.

In the end, they said it was up to Nellie to do whatever she felt was best and she decided she should go as she would be chaperoned. In truth, she relished the idea of spending more time with James and seeing the inside of a hotel bedroom fascinated her greatly.

'Excellent,' was his response. 'Now, you'll need to have some more formal clothes and a suitcase of course. I doubt you have a suitcase, do you?' Nellie shook her head.

'Never had cause to use one,' she replied.

'I'll bring one of ours. We have several in the trunk room. Mrs Wilkinson will select a suitable one for you.'

'And will you say who it's for?'

'Of course not. Don't want her knowing our business, do we? Now, if you go down to Wright's store, where we get the maids' uniforms, they have ready-made skirts and blouses and you'll need a jacket. Put them on my account. After all, it is for work.'

'If you're sure. Thank you. I've never had so many new things all at once.'

'You did a good job on those cups, by the way. I think they'll go well. Now, go and get your clothes sorted, in case they need altering. We shall leave on Monday morning and take the train up to Manchester.'

* * *

The next few days provided Nellie with a great deal of anxiety along with excitement. Would she know how to behave properly? She didn't want to let James down. She was looking forward to sharing meals with him and being able to chat in a relaxed way. She was finding it easier to call him James now, even in public. She packed the borrowed case and then unpacked it.

Her mother gave her a number of things to put inside it, which Nellie later removed. And then decided perhaps she should take them. She had only one decent pair of shoes, which she would wear to travel anyway. She packed the rag her mother had given her to polish the shoes. She also decided to travel in the new skirt, blouse and jacket.

'My, my, don't you look smart,' George, the gatekeeper, said as she arrived at work on the Monday morning. 'You look like one of them now. Them upstairs.'

Nellie blushed.

'I'm still the same Nellie. Just a bit smarter.'

'Good for you, girl. It's nice to see you getting on so well.'

Nellie had a window seat and watched as the fields rushed by. She had never realised there were so many cows in the countryside. Though she was slightly disappointed that they weren't talking to each other, she enjoyed the journey greatly. James was busy with papers from his briefcase, or so it seemed. In truth he was watching his companion. Mrs Wiley, his secretary, kept quiet and read a book.

He delighted in her delight as she saw new things. He could see her quick mind taking in everything she saw and somehow, looked as if she were filing away each new bit of information for a later date.

She was a remarkable woman, yes, truly now she was a woman. His mind was suddenly crystallised. She was his woman, or so he hoped. When they arrived in Manchester, she looked around with renewed interest.

'It isn't all that different to the Potteries, is it? But it's cleaner air cos it doesn't have all the kilns and chimneys belching out dirty smoke. There's some posh shops, but I expect we have those as well.'

'We'll go straight to the hotel and leave our bags and then on to the first call. You'll have to manage your bag yourself, I'm afraid. I have the samples case to carry as well as my own things. Unless you'd prefer me to call for a porter?'

'I can manage easy, thanks. It isn't too heavy. I'm used to carrying much more than this.'

They called at several large stores during the afternoon and listened to the buyers' comments about the new lines. James had brought pictures of the more traditional patterns, but it was the new pieces that excited them most. A number of good orders had been placed in addition to the more conventional designs. They had dinner at the hotel in the evening and felt buoyant at their success. Mrs Wiley retired to her room early.

'I'm not sure my father is in favour of this move to change from tradition but he sees the sense of moving forward. We won't stop doing the usual things because they will always sell. So, how do you feel about your first success and your first trip away?'

'I feel as if I'm floating on clouds. I love my room here. I can't believe all that space is just for me to use. And a proper bathroom. And the lovely things the buyers were saying and some of the ideas they gave me. I was nervous when they asked me questions but I felt as if they were pleased with my answers. I'm really looking forward to trying out some more ideas when we get back.'

'You did really well. I knew it would be a good idea to bring you with me. Nellie, my dear.' He reached over and took her hand. She glanced round to see if anyone was watching, but most people seemed to be concentrating on their meals.

'I can't believe you're the same shy little thing who looked up at me from your bench all that time ago. You looked so terrified, I wanted to pat you on the shoulder right away and tell you not to be afraid and that everything was all right. When I discovered you'd left, I was very disappointed. Then you turned up as a maid at our home. I could hardly believe it.'

'You mean to say you really remembered me from that first day? Why? I was just a paintress at one of the benches.'

'I can't say why. Perhaps it was fate. Something must have told me you were going to be important to us. To me. Nellie, I have been thinking of you such a lot lately.' He squeezed her hand. 'Nellie, would you do me the honour of marrying me?'

'Marry you? Me?'

He pretended to look under the tablecloth and Nellie giggled. 'There isn't another Nellie at our table is there? Well, what do you say?'

'I don't know. I mean, our families are worlds apart. With your background you could have anyone. Besides, your parents would never accept me into the family. Mrs Wilkinson would have a duck fit and Ethel and Clara would do nothing but snigger. How could I live like that?'

'We could get a place of our own somewhere. Just the two of us.'

'I'd like that.'

'Is that a yes then?'

'I don't know. I mean I'd have to think about it.'

'You do care for me, don't you? I believe I love you. Yes, I do, I know I love you. You're so sweet, honest and clever. And a beautiful woman as well. What more could I ask for?'

'But s'pose your family hate the idea? They might, you know, cut you off.'

'And you couldn't love me then? If I

was disinherited?'

'Don't be daft. As if that would make any difference. My parents have never had two pennies to rub together but they've stuck it out. It's just that I never dreamed you'd ask me to actually marry you. Not really. I might have dreamed about it once. Like a princess being asked to marry a handsome prince in the stories I tell little Lizzie.

'You mean the not-so-little Lizzie, now she's at school.' They both laughed together. 'And can you think of me as your handsome prince with you in the role of princess?'

'Doubt I'll ever be anything like a princess.'

'You will. On our wedding day.'

'If I say yes, you mean.'

'I shall keep pestering you till you do.'

'Why are you so good to me? To all of us?'

'Because you're going to make us a fortune with your clever designs.'

'I was thinking about that. We need

some more unusual shapes for the cups and plates. Could square shapes be made?'

'Yes. But I need an answer to my question.'

'Yes, please, James. Of course I'd love to marry you.'

'Oh Nellie, that's wonderful. We'll announce the news as soon as we get back and arrange the wedding immediately. There's no need for a long engagement, is there?'

'None at all. But you do realise, if we rush to get married everyone will think we had to get married.'

'Then they'll soon see they were wrong, won't they?'

The rest of the evening was spent discussing plans. Where would they live until they could afford somewhere of their own? Where the honeymoon would be? Nellie favoured Rhyl after her one trip there. James preferred the idea of a South Coast resort.

'But we have to tell our parents first off,' she said anxiously.

She knew her own parents would be delighted at the prospect of having the son of a factory owner for their daughter.

James's parents would hate the idea of having a paintress from their own factory as a daughter-in-law. She was right on both counts. They told her parents as soon as they returned.

James broke the news to his parents at dinner later that evening.

'I take it this is some sort of joke?' his mother said in a cold voice.

'She's the best you can do?' suggested his father. 'If you've got the child into trouble, I'll pay her off. Make sure she's got enough to look after the brat.'

'How dare you! Both of you. Nellie is a wonderful girl. I love her and no, I have not got her into trouble, as you put it. I shall marry her and if you don't like it, then we won't invite you to the wedding.'

'James! How can you bring us down like this? There are dozens of respectable girls who'd give anything to marry you. You have a position to keep up. A status. You're respected in this town, as is your father and all the family. People will talk.'

'Because I'm marrying the girl I love and a very talented one at that? Excuse me.' He threw his napkin on to the table and left the room.

His parents continued to debate the horrors of the situation as they saw it, long after the meal was finished.

'I shall disinherit him if he goes ahead,' Mr Cobridge said.

'But you can't. How will you manage without him? He's been practically running the factory since you've been unwell.'

'We've got managers in the various departments. I'll soon pick up the reins again.'

'And these new lines he says are so popular. Who will organise them? Not that I like them myself. Very crude.'

'As are most of today's youth. What a mess. Don't worry. The girl will soon drop him once she knows he'll be cut off without a penny.'

'I'm not so sure of that. But we shall see.'

The gossip found its way down to the kitchen.

' 'Ere, have you heard the latest? His lordship . . . the young one . . . wants to marry someone from the factory. The parents are furious. Any idea who it might be?' Ethel was grinning with delight. 'Her ladyship won't like it one bit. They both looked pretty grim at the table. He got up and stomped out of the house. Didn't even wait for pudding. Wonder if Mr James will really go ahead with his plans with his parents being like they are?'

'Bet it's that Nellie. Always was pushing herself at him. That painting and stuff she did.'

'You might be right. Keep listening when you can. We need to find out.'

★ ★ ★

'Ooh, our Nellie, well done,' was her father's response to the news. 'Now this family's really on the up.'

'Don't be silly, Dad. James thinks his father will disown him. We shall be looking for somewhere to live. He might even have to find another job. Well, both of us will.'

They began to discuss the wider implications. It was Nan who realised that once Nellie had left home, their own finances would be severely affected.

If she no longer lived at home, her wages wouldn't be helping support the family. Though she was delighted her daughter had found a man to love, she was going to miss her in more ways than one.

'Where do you think you might live?'

'I don't know, Mum. I just don't know. But if James is giving up everything for me, it must prove he really does love me, mustn't it?'

'Love? You can just forget all that nonsense. What you need is a decent home to bring up the kids. I presume you are expecting?' Enoch snapped at his daughter.

'Dad,' she said in horror. 'Course I'm not. James hasn't been anywhere near me. What do you think I am?'

'Enoch!' her mother exclaimed. 'I've brought our Nellie up to be a good girl. How could you say something like that?'

'Well, they can't live here with us. There isn't room.'

'We wouldn't think of it,' Nellie retorted.

The thought of James in these surroundings was almost laughable. She could hardly wait for the next day to hear how he'd got on with his parents. But she faced it with great trepidation. It could never be welcome news.

Family Woes For James

As she walked along the corridor to her little room at the factory, she heard raised voices coming from Mr Cobridge's office. She couldn't quite hear what was being said and decided she didn't want to hear.

She settled down to try and draw, but her mind was flying all over the place. She was waiting for James to come to his office.

It was almost an hour later when he finally arrived, looking pale and very weary. She left her chair and went to him.

'James, you look terrible. I take it you didn't give them popular news.'

'We're in trouble, Nellie. I've been walking around for most of night, trying to think. My parents were furious.

Father says he's cutting me out of his will and if we still plan to go ahead with our marriage, I'm to leave the factory immediately.'

'Then we can't go ahead. You can't marry me. There's far too much for you to lose.'

'I shall marry you, Nellie, if you'll still have me that is. Can you marry a poor man who has been used to having every comfort in life? A man who is useless at doing anything for himself? I don't even know how to make a cup of tea. I've never had to do it.'

'James, I can't let you do this. You are the heart and soul of Cobridge's. All your ideas are what make it successful. How often has your father been here lately?'

'Only because he's been unwell. He's looking ill today, but he came in despite that. It's still his factory. He took over from his father and continued to grow its good reputation. Don't you want to marry me if I'm a pauper?'

'It makes no difference to me, James.

I love you but I can't let you give up everything just for me. I'm not worth it. I'll leave. Maybe now I shall be able to get a job somewhere else. I know I can do designs that are popular.'

'You're right, Nellie Vale. You have got a talent we can use. We'll both find jobs somewhere else. But for now, we'll say nothing more. We'll get married in secret and then tell them later. Is that all right with you? Will you be disappointed if we don't have a big wedding?'

'If you're sure? And no, I'd be happier not to have a big wedding. I'd be embarrassed and my dad would make a fool of himself for sure. It's very romantic . . . a secret wedding.'

'I'll fix it up. Get the licence and everything. You're wonderful, Nellie Vale, and I love you.'

★ ★ ★

It was a difficult week, keeping their plans a secret and trying to work normally. The atmosphere at work was very tense. A week later, Nellie went to work wearing her smart skirt and jacket, telling her mother that they had a meeting.

She felt bad about not inviting her mother to her own wedding, but it was all for the best. She and James met at the registry office and the short, formal little ceremony united them in marriage. James slipped on the wedding ring. Afterwards, he gave her a silver chain so she could hang it round her neck, inside her clothing so nobody could see it. They remained apart for several more days.

'It doesn't feel like we're married at all,' Nellie murmured the following Friday. A weekend without seeing James was looming. 'Me going back to my parents and you continuing to live at your parents' home.'

'You're right. Maybe if they see we're actually married, they will relent and it won't be so bad. Besides, I want to be with you. Properly with you. I can't wait any longer. I want you to come home with me tomorrow. I'll call for you after lunch and you can come to Cobridge House for afternoon tea.'

'Really? But that might mean the end of everything for you with your own parents.'

'So be it. You'll come?'

'I suppose we have to face up to it sometime.'

'Two o'clock tomorrow then. And you must put on your wedding ring.'

'I'm scared, James.'

'So am I. But we shall be together at last.'

Nellie hardly slept that night. All the evening, her mother had been asking what was wrong.

'You look terrible, Nellie. Are you feelin' poorly?'

'No, Mum. I'm all right. Just got to think about summat.' Summat? A word she needed to forget. There were so many things she had to forget if she were to be the sort of wife James should have.

'Only if there's something wrong, you should come out with it.'

'It's all right, Mum. Really.' She felt her ring round her neck and wondered how they were going to take the news. She still had to face telling them that she was married. Though it was something different from what James was having to deal with, they would be disappointed not to have a celebration of the occasion.

Besides, her mother would never consider them to be properly married without a ceremony in the chapel. 'I'm going to have an early night. It's been a busy week.'

Despite her words, sleep was a long time coming. She tried not to toss and turn and disturb Lizzie who lay beside her. How many more nights would she be sleeping here? She shivered with some apprehension.

Tomorrow, she had to face Mr and Mrs Cobridge as their daughter-in-law. She was now Mrs Cobridge herself. *Nellie Cobridge* she repeated over and over again, trying to get used to the sound of it.

She helped her mother to clean the house next morning. It kept her busy and her mind slightly occupied. While they were having dinner, lunch as she should think of it in future, she announced that she was going out that afternoon.

'James is going to take me out for tea. I'm not sure when I shall be back.'

'That's nice, dear. I'd been wondering if everything was all right between you. Only you haven't said much lately. We thought you might be making plans but you haven't told us anything.'

'It's fine, Mum. I need to go and get ready now, so Lizzie and Ben, you help Mum with the washing up.'

She went upstairs and put on her best clothes. She brushed her hair till it shone and coiled it neatly. It made her look a bit older she thought. She bit her lip.

Should she wear her hat? She only had the one she wore for chapel and it didn't go with this outfit. She heard a knock at the door and decided it was too late anyway. She rushed down but she had been beaten to the door by her mother.

'Won't you come in, Sir?' she was asking. Nellie kept her fingers crossed that he would say no. She was tense enough without having her family asking awkward questions.

'It's all right. I'm here,' she said breathlessly. 'We need to be off, Mum, thanks.'

James smiled and nodded.

'Thank you, Mrs Vale, but we should go. Nice to see you and I hope your health is greatly improved.'

'Oh, it is. I'm ever so much better. I'm taking the medicine regular like, and eating better, like your doctor told me.'

'Good. Very good. Come along then, Nellie. Let's be on our way.'

'Thank you for not going inside. My mum's suspecting things are wrong and she'd be pumping you for answers.'

'Where's your wedding ring?' he asked, taking her hand. They stopped and she took it from round her neck and slipped it onto her finger.

'Feels funny there. I'm not used to it.'

'From now on, you'll be wearing it right there so you'd better get used to it. Are you ready for this, Mrs James Cobridge?'

'No,' she squeaked as they turned into the drive. 'Are you sure, James?'

'Quite sure. Come on.'

'Through the front door?' she whispered, pulling back and remembering her first visit to this house.

'Of course through the front door. From now on you are one of the family.' He took her arm and led her into the drawing room.

His parents were waiting there.

'Oh, it's you,' Mrs Cobridge said in a cold voice. 'I wondered whom he was bringing to tea.'

'Mother, Father, I'd like you to welcome my wife, Mrs Nellie Cobridge. Nellie, my parents.'

Timidly, she stepped forward and held out her hand to James's mother.

'Your what?' exploded his father.

'My wife. Nellie and I were married a couple of weeks ago.'

'You young fool! Well, you know what I said. It still stands. You can pack up your things and get out of this house.'

'I thought you might say that. I packed a suitcase earlier. I'll send for the rest of my things later. I love Nellie and I'm proud she accepted me as her husband.'

His new wife flashed him a grateful smile.

'I'm sorry, Nellie,' Mrs Cobridge said in a more gentle voice. 'James was warned what would happen. We simply cannot change our minds. You may wait in the hall for him to pack. I assume you have made some arrangements to find somewhere to live?'

'Not exactly, ma'am. We hoped that you would be pleased for us, once you knew we were wed.'

'And would you still have married him if you knew he would be penniless?' asked Mr Cobridge.

'I did suspect it might happen, and yes, of course I'd have married him. I love him. Being poor is nothing new to me.'

She held her head high now and spoke without fear. James had given her the confidence to speak out bravely to her former employers. She saw them for the snobs they were and was glad that James had a better character than his parents.

'And you'll need a new job. I don't want either of you in my factory.'

'We'll call on Monday for our personal things and then you need never see us again.' White-faced, James was stifling his emotions. Nellie could see he was deeply upset but he would never show it to his parents. There was a tap at the door.

'Are you ready for tea now?' asked Mrs Wilkinson. Her face was a picture as she saw Nellie and James standing

247

side by side. 'Nellie? What are you doing here?'

'Mrs Wilkinson. My wife and I will not be staying for tea after all. Thank you.'

As they left the room together, Nellie felt consumed by a fit of giggles. She could hardly keep her face straight as she murmured goodbye. She stood at the bottom of the stairs while James went to fetch his suitcase.

Mrs Wilkinson walked past her and stopped. She glared at Nellie, but decided to say nothing. She was after all, a model housekeeper and it did not do to pass comment on the affairs of her employers.

Nellie and James walked down the drive and out into the tree-lined road.

'Won't you miss living in this lovely place?' Nellie asked shyly.

'A little. More to the point, where are we going to live? I have some money saved. I was going to buy a car, you may remember. But it certainly isn't enough to buy a house. We can live off it for a little while but neither of us has a job now. For the weekend, let's go to the hotel. We can call it our honeymoon. Not quite what we were planning, but everything is changed now.'

'I can't just go to the hotel. Don't forget, we haven't told my parents yet.'

'Let's go and do it now. I hope their reaction to our marriage is a bit better than my parents'. You can collect what you need for the weekend and we'll start to make our plans for the future.'

★   ★   ★

Hand in hand, they knocked at the door of her home.

'Mum, Dad, can we come in?'

'Don't be daft. Course you can. Is there something wrong? Why is Mr James carrying a suitcase?'

The family were all sitting round the table. Nellie drew a deep breath.

'James and I are married.'

She held out her hand with the wedding ring on to show them. 'We were married a couple of weeks ago, but wanted it kept a secret till we could tell you all.'

'Oh, Nellie, love, Mr James. That's wonderful, but why do it all in secret? Oh dear, that means our Lizzie can't be a bridesmaid and we didn't even get a wedding breakfast.'

'I'm sorry, Mum, Dad. But it was a bit tricky. You see, James's parents threatened to cut him off if we went ahead. We hoped that when they could see how happy we are, they might change their minds.'

'I take it they didn't?' Enoch said looking at the suitcase.

'I'll put the kettle on,' Nan said. It was her universal panacea for any problems. Everything could be solved with a cup of tea. 'Come and sit yourselves down. We've got a lot to talk about.'

'We're going to stay at the hotel for the weekend. It will be our honeymoon,' James said firmly. He was determined that he and his bride would be alone for at least a couple of nights. 'We shall collect our things from the factory on Monday and begin our search for new jobs.'

'You mean you've been sacked from your own father's factory?' Nan said in horror.

'I'm afraid so. It's a total separation.'

'But how will they manage?'

'We shall have to wait to see. Now, I could really do with that cup of tea.'

'Yes, Sir. Right away.'

'And please, stop calling me *sir*. My name is James. I'm your son-in-law.'

Nellie saw Lizzie working up to whole series of her questions and took the child's hand.

'Come and help me pack some things, Lizzie. I'm going on a little holiday.'

'To the seaside? Can I come?'

'No. Not the seaside. But maybe one day, we can go to the seaside again.'

'When?'

'You'll have to wait and see.'

Nellie had nothing special to wear.

No trousseau or new things like most brides. Everything had happened too quickly. She still had her borrowed suitcase and packed her things into it.

She carefully folded her birthday dress, as she called it, and hoped that would do for dinner that night. She gave a quiver of excitement. She was going on her honeymoon. Now her life was truly changing.

*   *   *

For Nellie, the two nights spent in a small hotel quite close to her home, were complete bliss. James had taken great care of her, making sure she was comfortable and at ease.

Over breakfast on Monday morning they had to face the reality of their situation.

'We should go to the factory and collect our things. I want to gather up all your drawings. I'm not leaving any of them for someone else to use. And I have a number of personal items in my office that I want to keep.'

'But the drawings really belong to the company. I was paid to do them and . . .'

'They have the designs for the items for which we have orders. If they want more of the same, then they have to get in someone else or commission you to do some more. It will cost them serious money in either case.'

'But where are we going to put everything? We can't take it to the hotel. There's scarcely room to move as it is.'

'You make a good point. I'll get it packed into boxes and leave it at the lodge for now. We'll have to find somewhere to stay. The money will soon be gone if we stay on at the hotel, however cheap it is.'

Nellie was too happy to worry. She had James to do the worrying now. Somehow, everything would be all right.

'Do you think your father will be at the factory? I don't think I want to run into him.'

'He may be. Don't worry, little wife. I'll always look after you.' He took her hand and she felt a warm glow of love run through her body.

'I like being married to you, James.'

'Just as well. You're in it for life. Come on now. You agreed to 'better or for worse'. Let's hope that this bit is the worst we'll have to face. Let's get our coats and go and face the factory.'

It felt very odd to be going into the staff entrance and have the lodge keeper doff his cap instead of asking to search her bag. James held her hand as he saw her looking worried as they went up the stairs and into the office corridor.

There was nobody around and they went into his office. He had picked up one of the china crates on his way up and began to pack it with his things. Folders and files went in, though he put to one side the relevant files with the orders in them. He would pass that to his father's secretary to sort out.

His leather desk set, a gift from his parents when he started at the factory joined the growing heap of things. Nellie went into her little room and collected her brushes, paint tile and all the other things she had been using to create her designs, as James had instructed.

She picked up her collection of drawings and paintings and a pile of plain paper. She would need that if she was going to do any more work.

'I think that's it. Look, I really need to hand over the files and order books to the secretary. I must make sure everything is clear. Can you amuse yourself for the next hour or so?'

'Would you mind if I go down to the decorating shop? I'd like to say goodbye to Vera and some of the girls. I also thought I could ask her if she knows of any lodgings going. Might be worth it.'

'If you don't mind a few jokes at your expense. I suspect we are the subject of all the gossip going.'

'You know, I might actually enjoy it. Now I have you behind me, I have a lot more confidence.'

'Good for you. Come back here when you've had enough.'

Nellie went down the stairs and out into the yard. She crossed over, lifting her skirt to avoid the puddles and stepping carefully so she didn't ruin her shoes.

The outside stairs to the decorating shop seemed so very familiar and she almost felt wistful at the thought that this would be the last time she ever climbed it.

'Well look what the cat brought in,' called Florrie as she entered the shop. The rows of girls looked up from their benches. 'Lady Muck has come to see us.'

'Florrie, working hard as ever I see,' Nellie said with a bright smile. She nodded at some of her old friends and stopped at her former work place. 'Hello, Vera, Maggie. How are you?'

'This is a bit of a surprise,' Vera said. 'Are any of the rumours true then?'

'What rumours would they be?'

'A little dickey bird said you'd had to

get yourself hitched.'

'I am married, yes. But through choice, not necessity.'

'And is the lucky man who we think it is?'

'Unlucky if you ask me. Hear his dad's disinherited him. Bet you didn't expect that, did you, Nellie Vale?' Florrie couldn't resist being her usual, catty self.

'As a matter of fact, it was on the cards all along. But we decided to go ahead anyway.'

'So you have got wed to Mr James?' Vera asked.

Nellie nodded and smiled.

'Well done, ducks. I always knew he'd taken a shine to you. So where are you going to live, if he's been chucked out?'

'Can we have a private word, Vera? I don't want everyone to hear.'

'You go outside and wait. I'll join you in a minute.'

'Cheerio, everyone. I may see some of you again. Who knows what will happen in the future?' She walked out and heard a loud buzz of conversation as she shut the door. 'That's given them something to talk about,' she smiled.

'Right now. What did you want to say?' Vera asked.

'I wondered if you know of any cheap digs? Just temporary, like. Our place is too little and full to bursting anyway. Once we've both got jobs, we'll look for somewhere more permanent.'

'As it happens, our Kathleen's left home. She's getting wed herself and she's moved to their new place to get it decorated and everything. Lucky girl. You could have her room for a bit. Just to tide you over. It's got a bed in it, but that's about all. She's taken the chest of drawers and all her stuff.'

'Vera, you're a treasure. Are you sure you don't mind?'

'No. Glad to help. My old man will be pleased to have a bit of extra cash as well. When do you want to move in?'

'Tomorrow?'

'Right you are. I'll put on a bit of supper, being as it'll be your first night.

After that, you'll have to fend for yourselves. You can have the use of the kitchen and that, but I can't cook regular for the boss, now can I?'

'He's not like a boss. He's really very nice.'

'I should hope so seeing as how you've wed him. I'll have to get back now. Don't say owt to the others. They'll think I'm trying to suck up to the bosses. Won't do me any good at keeping them in line.'

James had mixed feelings about the arrangements but decided they had little choice until they had jobs. That was the next priority. They went back to the hotel, carrying Nellie's drawing and painting materials, having left everything else at the lodge.

He didn't want to talk about his meeting as his father had insisted on seeing him. He had tried to talk him out his plans and more or less suggested he abandoned Nellie and came to his senses.

'I shall buy the 'Evening Sentinel'

and see if there are any jobs advertised. Don't look so worried. I'm sure we shall soon find something. My experience is extensive for my age and you are good enough to work anywhere that does hand painting.'

Two days later, their luck turned. One of their rival companies was looking for a skilled paintress and also a manager of the glazing department. His father had insisted he did most of the jobs in the factory before he began work as the main manager so he had the right knowledge. It was messy work and he began to come home with crusts of white glaze round the bottoms of his trousers and shoes.

'I'll give him one thing,' Vera said to Nellie over the dishes, 'he's not afraid of hard work. I'm quite surprised. Didn't think he had it in him.'

James found life at Vera's difficult and very different from anything he had ever experienced. He hated going up the yard to an outside toilet and washing at the kitchen sink.

'Is this one of our company houses?' he asked after a few days.

'It certainly is. And lucky we are to have it.'

'I need to do something about it. It's unthinkable that people have to live like this with no bathroom and an outside toilet.'

'And just what do you think you can do?' Nellie asked. 'You don't have a company any more.'

'You don't need to tell me.'

'I'm sorry. It's all my fault, isn't it?'

'No, Nellie. You must not say that, ever. It was my choice and I'm lucky to have you. Now, are we going to see your parents this evening? At least we can have a bit of a walk and give Vera some space.'

'I'm glad you came, Nellie. There's a letter come for Mr James. I was going to get our Joe to bring it round later.'

'A letter for me?' James looked puzzled. 'Who would write to me here?' He took the envelope. 'Oh. It's Mother's writing. What does she want?'

He tore open the envelope and read the brief message. 'She says my father's ill. Very ill. She wants me to go and visit. I don't know, after last time.' He slumped down onto a chair looking the most unhappy Nellie had ever seen him.

'You must go, James. She wouldn't ask unless he was really ill. You know he hasn't been well for a long time.'

'I suppose so.'

'Go and see him right away. It's still quite early. Go round now. I'll walk back to Vera's and wait there.'

'Won't you come with me?'

'No. You should go alone. We don't want them to think you're afraid of seeing them.'

'Are you sure you don't mind?'

'Of course not. Now go. You'd never forgive yourself if he really was at death's door.'

'Maybe. But don't forget, it's his choice, not mine. We gave both of them the chance to accept us.'

★　★　★

Nellie waited anxiously for James to come back to Vera's. She sat by the fire, wishing he'd return and she would know what was wrong. Suppose he stayed there? Suppose he decided he couldn't face living with her any longer? She had worked herself into quite a state by the time she heard him walking up the path. She rushed to open the door before he made a noise and woke the others. He looked very pale and drawn and wearier than she had ever seen him before.

'Tell me, James. What did they say?'

'Father is ill. Really ill, He can no longer work at the factory. According to Mother, there are very many problems and they have asked me to go back and work there. Sort things out before it goes bankrupt.'

'Is it really that bad?'

'I don't know. I don't know if they are just trying to make me feel guilty. But it's their fault, not mine. They only had to say they accept you as my wife and I'd go back like a shot.'

'I think you should go back and run the factory. After all, it is your inheritance, even if your father has written you out of his will.'

'But unless they accept you as their daughter-in-law, I don't want to have any more to do with them.'

'At least go in and see what's happening. You don't have to go to work on Saturday so why not call in then?'

'You really think so?'

She nodded.

'Very well, I'll do as you say. But if you're not welcome in the house, we'll have to stay here for a while longer. That might be difficult for Vera if I'm back being the boss again.'

'We'll face that when the time comes.'

'You're wonderful, Nellie Cobridge. I just wish my awful parents could see it.'

Settling An Old Score

For the next few weeks, James went to the factory each day and came home looking exhausted. He had handed in his notice at the rival factory. There was little peace or privacy at Vera's and it was beginning to take its toll.

'I think we need to get somewhere of our own to live,' James announced. 'I shall have to stay running the factory so at least we have money again.'

'It isn't easy finding anywhere to rent. You have a perfectly good home. Why don't you go back to stay with your parents?'

'You know why. I can't take you there and I'm not going without you.'

When James came home from work the next day, grim faced, Vera handed him a note.

'What's this?'

'I don't know. Read it and you'll find out.' He took it up to their room and sat on the bed. He read the words with disbelief.

My dearest James,

I'm so sorry to leave you like this but I can see what it's doing to you. I'm holding you back and you need to be with your parents again, especially as your dad is so poorly. It's for the best. I'm moving back home and you can go and live where you belong. I'll always love you and thank you for the happiest weeks of my life.

Your own, Nellie.

'You silly goose. Oh, Nellie, as if I'd ever want to change anything. You are more important than any big house or factory or anything.'

'Then you'd best go and tell her. You know where she is.' Vera had been standing outside their door.

'Thanks, Vera. You're right. You're a good friend.'

James rushed round to the Vale house

and banged on the door. Nan came to open it.

'It's no good. She doesn't want to see you. She won't tell me anything.'

Nellie was sitting close to the fire, eyes red and clutching a mug of tea in her hands, as if she were trying to drag some warmth from it.

'Go away. You don't need me in your life. You'll be much better without me.'

'I love you, Nellie. We can fight this. If you leave me, we shall both be unhappy for the rest of our lives. You're worth more to me than all the big houses in the world.'

'But your parents won't ever believe it,' she sobbed.

'You're being daft, our Nellie,' Enoch said from his chair. 'You've got a good man who says he cares. Stop behaving like an idiot and go home with him.'

'Some home we've got. A tiny bedroom in someone else's house when he's used to a luxury mansion with a fleet of servants to look after him. You should see his face when he has to walk up the yard to go to the netty.' She gave a feeble grin and James took her hand. She allowed him to pull her up and he wrapped his arms round her.

★　★　★

A few days later, James's father died. There was a massive funeral four days later for this well-known local figure. The factory was closed for the afternoon and all the staff were expected to attend the church service.

James insisted that Nellie should accompany him and he walked between his mother and wife, as chief mourners. Mrs Cobridge refused to say a word to her daughter-in-law, but Nellie behaved with such dignity that James felt very proud of her.

The invited guests came back to the house, where a funeral wake had been laid on. There was a moment's strain when Ethel handed a cup of tea to Nellie and giggled out loud. Nellie glared. She had not forgotten that it was this girl who had contributed to her being sacked.

'What am I going to do now, James?' his mother wailed after the guests had gone. 'I can't live all alone in this big place.'

'Then the answer is simple. Nellie and I will move back.'

'I don't want a maid of ours sitting at the dining table.'

'Then you'll have to live alone. Your choice. Come along, Nellie. We are not wanted here.' He tucked her arm into his and they walked out together. Nellie looked at him, wondering exactly what he was thinking. Men never cried of course but she couldn't really tell how deeply he felt about his father's death.

'Stop. Don't go.' Mrs Cobridge was standing by the door. She looks old, Nellie thought. Suddenly, the woman was looking worn and rather pathetic. They turned and clutching her husband's arm, Nellie walked back to the door with him.

'All right,' the woman said ungraciously. 'She can come. I can't live alone, but nor can I forget she was one of our maids.'

'She is your daughter-in-law. She is called Nellie. I want you to be kind to my wife. I want you to treat her as one of the family.'

'Very well. Please, will you stay here tonight, though? I'm frightened of being alone.'

'We'll come back tomorrow. You have Mrs Wilkinson and the maids in the house. You are not alone.'

'You'd better take your father's car. It is yours now, after all.'

'I thought nothing was to be mine any more?'

'I don't think your father ever changed his will. You will inherit everything. Once I've gone of course.'

Vera could hardly believe it when a car stopped outside her house. When James and Nellie got out, she guessed there were about to be some changes.

'How did it go? Back at the house, I mean?'

'It was all right. Tense. Mrs Cobridge wants us to move back. She doesn't like being alone.'

'What, both of you?'

'Of course. You didn't think I'd ever go without my wife, did you?'

'Well, I'm happy for you. But I shall have to get another lodger.'

'And I have every intention of making these houses better places to live. You'll have to decide if you want a bathroom upstairs or down. You'd lose the little bedroom, but I think it would more than make up for it.'

They ate a cold supper and went to bed early. It had been a stressful day and tomorrow, a new life would begin. After breakfast, they went up to their little room for the last time.

'You ready for this, Nellie?'

'I suppose so. Bit of change isn't it?'

'Life moves on. Now, I'll begin taking things down to the car.'

Vera came into the room. 'Posh, isn't

he, with a car an' all?' Vera looked troubled. 'How will you manage with her Ladyship? I mean, you were a maid in the house and now you're going in as the lady of the house.'

'I don't know. She clearly doesn't want me there, but James insists that it's both of us or none. It's Mrs Wilkinson troubles me most. She bosses everyone all the time. Even the family were told how to behave.'

'You finished packing?' James asked as he came back up the stairs.

'Just a couple more things to put in. Then there's the painting bits and bobs. I can't thank you enough, Vera. You've helped us when we most needed it.'

'Good luck, Nellie. I think you might need it.'

'I'll see you at work from time to time. I shall be working at the factory again from next week on. I'm going to be bringing some of the new lines in. James is putting me in charge so I'll be down to make sure you're doing what we want.'

'Whoever would have thought our shy little Nellie would be one of the bosses? Well, I'm going to be late for work. Hope the boss doesn't give me me cards.' They all smiled.

'Come on, Nellie. Let's go and sort ourselves out at Cobridge House. I thought we'd move into my old room, if that's agreeable to you. Or perhaps you'd prefer one of the guest rooms?'

'Goodbye, Vera, and thanks again.'

'Bye, love. Hope it goes all right.'

They drove away and Nellie found that tears were pressing the back of her eyes. It was as if she was mourning the loss of her old life and facing her new one with trepidation. They stopped the car outside the front door. James leapt out and rang the bell. Nellie began to collect her things, but James stopped her.

'We'll get the girls to unload the car. Come on. We'll see if Mother's finished breakfast.' He looked at his watch. Nine o'clock.

'She won't have finished yet. She

doesn't want it cleared before half-past most days.' James smiled at her. He knew what she was thinking. It used to be her job to clear the table. 'She was always quite charming on those days, when I was just a little maid. No wonder she's finding it difficult to see me as your wife.' He gripped her hand and tapped on the breakfast room door.

'Morning, Mother. We came early to get ourselves established. We need to go to the factory later. There's a lot to be done. Oh, good, there's some coffee left. Would you like some, Nellie?'

'I'm not much for coffee, but some tea would be nice.'

'Ring the bell and we'll get some brought in.'

'I can just as easily go to the kitchen . . . '

'Nonsense. Sit down and maybe you'd enjoy a slice of toast?'

Nellie sat down at the table with Mrs Cobridge for the first time in her life. The woman ignored her and watched as James poured his coffee. 'Did you sleep well, Mother?' he asked politely.

'Not really. I may need to go and lie down again. There are too many changes in my life, too quickly.'

'I expect you will need to accompany me to the solicitors this afternoon. We need to set things in place for the future.'

'I can't possibly go out. You will have to deal with it.'

'You will have things to sign. I'll ask him to come here. Three o'clock suit you?' He didn't wait for an answer.

Nellie watched the pantomime playing before her. James was so self-assured and knew exactly how to assume the role as head of the family.

Ethel came in and James looked straight at Nellie. He wanted her to give an order. She swallowed hard to push the nerves away.

'I'd like some tea, please, Ethel.'

'Right, Miss. Mrs. What do I call you?'

'Mrs Nellie will do nicely,' James told her.

His wife smiled as Ethel left the room. She liked the sound of that. 'Well, Mrs Cobridge is too confusing. We can't have two ladies with the same name in one household.'

His mother actually looked relieved. Perhaps Nellie's new title seemed less of a threat. 'We need to speak to Mrs Wilkinson too. Make sure she knows what's what now.' Nellie looked apprehensive. 'You know, the Dragon Lady,' he said gently. It always made her laugh and it relieved the growing tension.

'James. We only call her that in private,' she scolded.

'We are in private,' he replied, taking Nellie's hand comfortingly. It was certainly going to be an uphill struggle for acceptance.

'You wanted to see me?' Mrs Wilkinson said to Mrs Cobridge, with hardly a glance at Nellie.

'Yes,' James said. 'Mrs Nellie and I will be using my old room for the time being. We may move to one of the guest rooms later, when my wife has decided

276

how she would like it to be decorated. We shall be out for lunch but I'm arranging for our solicitor to call this afternoon. Please arrange for tea to be served at four, as usual. We will all be in for dinner this evening. I assume you will be in, Mother?'

'Of course. Where else would I go? Now I am a widow, few people will invite me out. I shall be dining in my room, Mrs Wilkinson. In fact, get the maids to bring a small table to my room. I expect to be spending a lot of time there in future.'

'Oh, Mother,' James said angrily. 'You could at least make some effort.'

The reading of the will took place in the drawing room. It was a simple transfer of the entire factory into James's name and the house and assets were also to be his. There was provision for his mother to live there for as long as she lived or wanted to stay. She also had a generous allowance.

The will had been written some years ago, well before James and Nellie had been married. It was fortunate for them that he had been too unwell actually to carry out his threats to change it all.

For Mrs Cobridge, life went on pretty much as it always had done. Her husband had often dined out without her and she had always organised her days as she wanted to.

★ ★ ★

The next weeks were difficult for Nellie. Whenever James was out, his mother would ask her to fetch things or go to the kitchen to bring tea to her.

Apart from the fact that she stayed in the room while tea was being drunk, she felt as if she were still a maid there. Mrs Wilkinson did treat her with a modicum of respect, though she frowned occasionally when Nellie asked for something, suggesting that there was still a little resentment.

She never mentioned it to James and he remained unaware that anything was ever wrong. She was happiest when she accompanied him to work at the factory.

Nellie's new design office was situated near to the decorating shops. Though she could have taken over James's old office when he moved into his father's, it was decided that it would be much more practical for her to be near her team of paintresses.

Her request for some new shapes to be made for plates and cups had been carried out. She worked with several geometric shapes which were becoming fashionable with the art deco movement.

It was three years since their marriage and modern styles were beginning to fill the shops. She had rivals in her designs, but she was still the only person making items in bone china.

'I do like these earthenware lines. In some ways, they hold the deeper enamel colours better. And there's some nice cream ware coming in. Clarice and Susie are at the top of that tree,' she told James. He watched her working with such pride. Her newly bobbed hair suited her perfectly and her smart clothes would allow her to go anywhere.

'I can't believe how much you've changed, Nellie. You're a bit like our china. You look delicate and fragile but there is surprising strength there. You seem like a completely new person. Still the same wonderful girl I married, but I hear you talking to the men as if you truly are in charge. I'll be redundant before I know it.'

'Don't be silly, James. They do what I tell them because of you. It's only because I'm your wife. They know that I'll tell you if anything is wrong and then their jobs will be at risk. I was wondering if we shouldn't branch out a bit.'

'What are you thinking of?'

'Well, we only make tableware. Basic stuff. Why don't we make tureens? Large jugs and vases? Bit more in the way decorative lines? Have you seen some of the pretty dishes that are coming into the shops?'

'I'll talk to the mould makers and the production managers. See what the difficulties are. Produce a few sketches to show me and them what you're thinking of.' She leaned down to the wide drawers beside her desk.

'Here're a few sketches I've done already.' She handed him a folder with a whole sheaf of different designs.

'Oh, Nellie, what would we do without you? I'm sure our recent success is down to you.'

'Good. I hope you all like them. Now, if I don't go into the decorating shop, we won't have anything ready for the next firing. I really will have to do something about Albert. He's a lazy blighter.'

'We can always find someone else if you don't think he's doing his job. Do you want me to speak to him?'

'Certainly not. I'm more than capable of sacking him if I think he needs it.'

The girls looked up as Nellie came

in. Most of them had accepted that she was now the power behind all the new designs.

Some of the older 'girls' hated the bold, brash colours and wanted to continue to paint the roses and other flowers they had been doing all their lives.

Many of them had been put to work on the transfer designs, where minimal hand painting gave added colour.

The fairy plates were still popular and photographic transfers were being developed. There were also several small sets of plates and bowls using similar patterns for children's ware. This too was proving popular and some of the girls were now working full time on these.

Nellie felt proud of the innovations, brought about by a more forward-thinking manager of the factory.

With James's support, she had accomplished so much. If only it was the same at Cobridge House. Hints had been made by her own family and several of their friends about providing an heir to Cobridge's. While James's mother still frowned at her on a daily basis, there was no way that she could ever spend her days at home. Besides which, it simply had never happened. She had never become pregnant.

Nellie glanced across at the window of Albert's office. As always, Florrie was sitting on his desk, her back to the window. Albert hadn't noticed Nellie's arrival in the workshop and was continuing to talk to the girl. More than girl these days, Nellie thought. She must be nearing forty by now but as Albert was in his fifties, she probably seemed young to him.

'How's life treating you, Nellie?' asked Vera as she passed her bench. She was the only one of them allowed to call her Nellie. If anyone else was overly familiar, Vera gave them the sharp end of her tongue. Even Florrie had stopped being catty to her, at least to her face. 'Can I have a quick word?'

'Of course. Nothing wrong, is there?'

They went out of the room to talk.

'Sorry, but I haven't seen you properly for ages and I wondered how you're going?'

'I'm fine thank you, Vera. And you?'

'Fine, ta. You can tell your husband how much we like our new bathroom. It'll be such a treat not to have to walk up the yard in the middle of winter. You know we've had the whole place decorated too? You'd scarce know us nowadays.'

'I'm glad to hear it. He always did want to improve the housing.'

'How about your lot? They doing OK?'

'Yes. They've got a new house, too. Our Joe's working on a farm out in the country. He's loving it. Mum's much better and at last Dad's got treatment for his hand. Much happier they are now. Is there anything else you wanted to say?'

'Not really. Well, I know I shouldn't tattle, but I think you need to watch Florrie. You know she's always had it in for you. I think she and Albert are up to something. Something more than, well, you know what.'

'Thanks for telling me. I have been concerned that Albert isn't doing his job as he should for a while. What's Florrie up to?'

'Nothing I can put my finger on. I think she's just frustrated that Albert hasn't left his wife for her. He's been promising for years but never does it.'

'I'll go and speak to him. I have several things to say anyway.'

They went back into the room and Vera settled back to work. Nellie looked at several of the girls at they worked and complimented some of them on their skills. They smiled back at her, respecting her because she had been one of them.

Florrie was still sitting on the desk, her legs crossed and giggling as Albert was paying more than a little attention to her. He saw Nellie coming and pushed Florrie away.

'Right then, Florrie, you'll do that for me, will you.'

'Certainly, Mr Albert. Right away.' She sniggered as she passed Nellie and gave an extra wiggle of the hips for Albert's benefit.

'Morning, Mrs Nellie,' he said obsequiously, almost bowing his head to her. 'How are we today?'

'What was Florrie really doing in here?'

'She just came in . . . I wanted her to do something. She'll see to it now.'

'She was sitting on your desk for at least fifteen minutes.'

'Oh, no. She just came in, just before you did.'

'Don't lie. I was in here earlier only you were so involved in doing whatever you were doing, you didn't notice. Don't forget I used to work here. It didn't pass unnoticed that she spent a considerable amount of her day sitting on your desk. What you choose to do outside work is up to you. But you are paid to manage.'

'You can't never complain about the numbers. I always get the orders out on time.'

'True, but if you can spend so much time chatting to your . . . whatever she is, I suggest you are under-worked. She is not paid to sit on your desk, so clearly she is not pulling her weight either. I shall be watching both of you very carefully from now on. I want individual numbers of every item painted by each worker for the next two weeks. Some designs take longer, so name whatever it is they are working on.'

'But that will take hours. I'll have to go round each bench at least once a day.'

'You mean you are not doing that already? You should be. It's part of every manager's job to know his workforce precisely and know what they are capable of. If you don't like it, you and Florrie will both be getting your cards at the end of next week.'

She stormed out of his office. She

saw one or two of the girls miming applause. She must have spoken louder than she realised. Florrie's bench was further away so undoubtedly, she would be going to speak to Albert as soon as she had left.

She shut the door and waited for a few moments before quietly pushing it open again and standing watching with her arms folded. She saw Albert telling Florrie the latest news and watched as she retreated quickly and went back to her bench, casting a glance of pure venom at Nellie.

One week later, Nellie actually found herself congratulating Albert on the greatly improved productivity in the department. Florrie's wage packet was somewhat lighter than the other girls at her bench. She was not used to working with any speed and let her anger show to the others.

The girls on her bench were a little afraid of her and soon, her wages improved by means of persuading each of the other girls to allot one piece of work each day to her total, thus depriving them of the benefit. They knew that Mr Albert would take it out on them if they didn't agree.

It was Vera who finally overheard the other girls talking and learned of Florrie's little scheme. She pondered over the problem, wondering if she should tell Nellie, but she didn't want to become known as a sneak. It would damage her own reputation.

She came up with the idea that the girls should take their finished ware to an unused side bench, each time they completed a dozen and there would be a chart they could tick off as they left it there.

'It'll make it easier for you and you'll be able to watch and see who takes what, won't you?'

'I s'pose it might work. But it'll mean somebody'll always be on the move.'

'Maybe. But it's good for us to move regular, like. Makes concentration better when we go back.'

They tried the scheme. Life for

Florrie became more difficult. She was unable to collect the pieces from the others without being noticed. Albert called her in at the end of the week.

'Now then, Florrie, what's going on? Your numbers are right down this week. The others at your bench are improved. How do you explain it?'

'Come on, Albert. What's a few pots between friends? Maybe I've been saving my energy for later.' She grinned and pushed herself towards him.

'What do you think you are doing?' roared Nellie from his office door. Neither had seen her come into the room and were unprepared for her outburst.

'I was just querying why her numbers were down, Mrs Nellie.'

'Didn't look much like it to me. I'm sick of this. Every time I come into this shop, that girl is dangling herself over your desk. That's it. You've had your warnings. You can both collect your cards. You'll get a week's pay in lieu of notice. Now, clear your desk and collect your personal possessions and leave.'

'You can't do this to me, Nellie,' Albert protested. 'I've got children to take care of. I've worked here for years. I'm too old to get another job anywhere.'

'Then it's a pity you didn't think of your children when you were flirting with Florrie. Don't think I don't know what's been going on all these years. Think yourself lucky someone hasn't told your wife, poor woman.'

She turned and swept out of the workshop. Florrie watched her go and stood in front of the rest of the girls.

'That madam can't treat us like this. She knows what it's like working in here. She got the sack herself at one time. We need to organise a strike against unfair dismissal. Are you with me, girls?' She began chanting 'Strike, strike, strike,' in a loud voice. Nobody joined in. 'Come on, you lot. You don't know when it might be your turn.'

'Shut up, Florrie. You've had it too easy for too long. It's not unfair dismissal, it's absolutely fair. You're nothing but a scheming strumpet who's got her come-uppance at long last.'

'I hate you lot. Mealy mouthed nobodies.' She picked up a glass jar and threw it onto the side bench where the lines of finished ware were awaiting collection. 'There. Now none of you will get full pay this week.' She grabbed her bag and paintbrushes and other bits from her bench and stormed out. There was a moment's silence before a couple of the younger girls began to wail.

'I've been working extra hard this week to earn something towards my wedding. Now it's all ruined.'

'I'll go and have a word with Mrs Nellie. Tell her what's gone down. Mebbe she'll be sympathetic.' Vera went out of the room.

'I'll be looking for a new manager in the department, Vera. I'd like to offer it to you. I know it means we shall be losing a talented paintress, but I think you'll manage the girls very well. What do you say?'

Overwhelmed at the offer, Vera agreed and it seemed the department would soon be flourishing under the new management. Nellie relaxed. All she needed to do now was to get the situation at home sorted out and her life would be perfect.

Mrs Cobridge had taken to her bed for large parts of the day. She claimed to be ailing and treated the maids far less kindly than before. There was in truth, little wrong with the woman, but it made Nellie and James's lives easier when they didn't have to face her miserable face across the dinner table.

'Don't worry about her, my dear,' James said quite regularly. 'It's her own fault that she can't accept you as a member of the family. If she wants to live the rest of her life as an embittered old woman, that's her choice. You and I have got our own lives to lead.'

'Now we're earning good money, do you think we can pay towards my little brother and sister to have a proper education? Lizzie's bright and she's nine now. I want her to have good chances in life. As for Ben, he's going the same way as Joe and skips school far too often. And as for our own? I wonder if he or she will have my artistic streak? It won't be long until we find out . . . '

'What do you mean?' James asked.

'I said, perhaps our own child will show their artistic side!'

'You're expecting a baby? Oh, my darling Nellie. Well done. Now we really do have a future of our own to look forward to. I love you, Nellie Cobridge.'

'And I you, James Cobridge.'

THE END

**FROM THIS DAY ON
WHERE THE HEART IS
OUT OF THE BLUE**

We do hope that you have enjoyed reading this large print book.

Did you know that all of our titles are available for purchase?

We publish a wide range of high quality large print books including:
Romances, Mysteries, Classics
General Fiction
Non Fiction and Westerns

Special interest titles available in large print are:
The Little Oxford Dictionary
Music Book, Song Book
Hymn Book, Service Book

Also available from us courtesy of Oxford University Press:
Young Readers' Dictionary
(large print edition)
Young Readers' Thesaurus
(large print edition)

For further information or a free brochure, please contact us at:
Ulverscroft Large Print Books Ltd.,
The Green, Bradgate Road, Anstey,
Leicester, LE7 7FU, England.
Tel: (00 44) **0116 236 4325**
Fax: (00 44) **0116 234 0205**

TRUTH, LOVE AND LIES

Valerie Holmes

Florence Swan's plan is to escape from Benford Mill School for young women before she is forced to work in their cotton mill. Naïve, ambitious and foolhardy, she ventures out on her own, her path crossing that of Mr Luke Stainbridge — a man accused of being mad. He has returned home from imprisonment in France to discover that his home has been claimed by an imposter. Together they find the truth, disproving clever lies, and discover life anew.